NOW IS THE TIME...

Jay Larkin

To C.
My Rock

CONTENTS

CHAPTER 1

Is this a mistake? Yolanda thought as she drove along the motorway under an ominous grey sky. *Should I have cancelled?* Even now, it wasn't too late to turn back. The elegant, sweeping lines of the Queen Elizabeth bridge rose before her like a piece of sculpture. Crossing the River Thames felt like the point of no return. Leaving London and her normal life behind, and entering... what? How fanciful. It was only a few days at the Kent coast. Hardly life changing. The sun came out as she drove across the wide expanse of the bridge, revealing blue sky, and she smiled in spite of herself. No turning back.

Yolanda checked the time. She'd set off later than planned, but after all, what was the rush? It wouldn't take her more than an hour to reach Westgate. She could pick up the Airbnb keys any time after three. She'd get coffee at the next service station. It was hard to turn off a habit, when the rest of her life was about deadlines and accounting for every minute of her time. This was a chance to chill out.

Sitting at a plastic table with a passable latte at three on a Monday afternoon wasn't usual for Yolanda. And she wasn't supposed to be alone. Claudia had let her down at the last minute. The trip was Claudia's idea. Yolanda's friends from work would be horrified; a precious few days off invariably involved an airport, guaranteed sun and serious partying. But Claudia wasn't like her colleagues.

They'd met at the art class. Yolanda loved art at school, but like all other hobbies, her mum had regarded it as a distraction. Yolanda must focus her efforts on a career. About a year before, after the breakup with Mark, she'd seen a flyer for a course at the Camden Arts Centre, and gone along on an impulse. Over the months, she got to know and like Claudia. At the end of the year, there was going to be an exhibition, her first opportunity to show her work.

That was the reason for the trip. Claudia suggested a week by the sea might give them ideas and inspiration. She knew the East Kent area, and told Yolanda there were natural elements nearby – sea, rocks countryside and white cliffs, as well as manmade structures like Canterbury Cathedral.

Claudia had an eight-year-old son, Joseph. Her mum had recently retired and was keen to look after him. Claudia had found a pleasant looking flat on Airbnb and they booked it for a week. Yolanda felt guilty taking the time off because they were busy at work, but they were always busy. Her law firm's culture cultivated the type of busyness that served to highlight the individual's importance and indispensability, rather than genuine achievement. But the day before, Claudia's mum had tripped and broken her ankle.

At first, Yolanda was disappointed, but didn't consider going by herself. However, the idea of a quiet break by the sea was appealing, and to her surprise, in the end she decided to go alone. She could always go back home if she got fed up. She'd been working long hours on an important case which was going to trial the following week. The team had hoped the case could be settled out of court, but in spite of all their efforts, the trial was going ahead. That would involve two weeks of intensive effort and even longer hours than usual.

Yolanda called Molly, who was to hand over the keys to the flat and arranged to meet her there at four. As she drove down the M2 and then the A299, the traffic thinned out. Yolanda noticed green fields by the side of the road and trees outlined against a blue. And over a low hill, a flash of deeper blue. The sea. This was an alien landscape to Yolanda. The places she knew best were the industrial northern town of her childhood, London's overwhelming presence and several interchangeable Mediterranean holiday resorts.

Yolanda couldn't remember her hard working mum ever taking a holiday, apart from Christmas Day. No one wanted their hair done on Christmas Day, but if they had, her mum would've opened the salon. One of the salons – there were four in total situated around Leeds and Bradford. When she was too young to be left alone, Yolanda was sent to her grandparents for the school holidays. Then as a teenager, she worked in the salon. She wasn't given a choice, though to be fair, she was paid the going rate. But her mum – Jackie's – financial success was hard won. Her creed was 'Work harder than anyone else', and she'd built up a lucrative business through sheer hard graft.

Yolanda was clever, quick, industrious and invariably among the top in her class. Her mum saw a bright future ahead, she had her daughter's path mapped out. Eventually Yolanda accepted a place to study law at a prestigious university in London. So here she was, at thirty-three, a lawyer in a prominent firm, Nelson Riggs, working long, stressful hours and getting well paid for it. She had a group of friends from work and university. Friends made out of propinquity, convenience. Claudia was the first friend she'd made out of a shared interest.

Yolanda turned off the motorway and drove on down quiet roads, through villages, rows of bungalows and pretty cottages. Then she crossed a humped railway bridge. This was Westgate-on-Sea. Past a parade of shops, onwards as far as she could go to the sea. She turned right into Sea Road, her destination. Few cars were parked on the quiet, wide road. An attractive group of four low rise buildings faced the sea. Ivyside was one of these

She got out of the car and crossed over the road to the sea. She sniffed the air self-consciously. Was sea air different from any other air? The outlook was prettier than she expected – than the photo on the website. A wide sweep of sandy bay edged with grass and shrubs. And so quiet, hardly anyone around.

Her heart rate slowed down perceptibly. She looked at her watch and saw a woman waiting, obviously Molly. After greetings were exchanged and Molly told her where to park. They took the lift to the first floor. The door opened into a small entrance hall and through to the main living room. Molly told Yolanda there was milk in the fridge and other basics in the kitchen cupboards. She showed her how the hot water, heating, and locks worked. A file of information about the flat and the local area lay on the kitchen countertop.

"I've got to dash to get the kids," said Molly, going out, "anything you need, give me a ring. I'm just around the corner."

Then she was gone and Yolanda was alone. This flat was larger than her one bed in West Hampstead, carved out of an old building. This was purpose-built, modern and well designed. It was simply, but comfortably furnished. And the view. The living room opened onto a small balcony overlooking the sea. The quiet road in between didn't detract from the effect.

Yolanda made a cup of tea, walked through the living room to the balcony and sat down. Soothing blues of sea and sky spread through her body, and her heartbeat slowed to a hypnotic pace. Tension flowed away. She noticed small sounds. The clunk of her mug on the slatted table. Her chair leg squeaking against the wooden balcony. Even the clink of her ring against the mug. A car driving along the road made her jump, the roar of its engine unnaturally loud. Her hearing hadn't become more acute – there was no background noise. No hum of traffic, screeching of brakes, hooting of car horns or voices of any kind. Just the tinkling of a fountain in the small garden below, and the wind rustling the leaves of the tree by its side.

She'd never experienced quiet like this in her London life. Her flat was located on a busy road, with twenty-four-hour shops and traffic day and night. In the office, others were always within earshot, and she'd learned to tune out colleagues' phone conversations in order to concentrate. The obligatory drinks nights in bars, were accompanied by a perfect cacophony of music, laughter, loud voices and the clash of glasses. To deal with the continual barrage of background noise, Yolanda like most city dwellers, had developed a protective filter that tuned out the surrounding sounds. It would be impossible to function without it. However, now there was no aural attack, the filter faded. It was a cliche, but she found the silence deafening. Unnerving. She was conscious of every tiny sound around her.

Again, her body relaxed, but part of her brain remained clenched like a fist. What was inside that tight, hard grip? Eyes closed, Yolanda tried to uncurl the mental fingers, but they wouldn't budge. As she gave up, her breathing deepened. On the verge of sleep, something slipped out. A murmur.

Is this what you want?

The unmentionable thought. The question never asked. The choice never faced.

A car door slammed. Voices rose. A dog barked. She sat up abruptly and rubbed her eyes. The filter returned. The question was gone.

◆ ◆ ◆

It was getting late and she was hungry. Yolanda had a good appetite in spite of years of suppression. Her mum, Jackie, survived on black coffee and cigarettes. She despised cooking, 'For housewives,' she said with a sneer. Before Yolanda even understood the term, she knew it wasn't a compliment. Without her hot lunch at school, she sometimes thought she'd have starved.

As soon as she could, Yolanda learned to make simple meals. All the girls took a short cookery course at school, which she loved. But to attend the after-school cookery club, she had to tell her mum she was doing extra maths, and hide or eat all the goodies she made. And of course, there was the weight issue. Jackie was whippet slim, 'There's no such thing as too thin,' was another of her sayings. As soon as Yolanda reached puberty, Jackie began to keep a critical eye on her daughter's figure. One of her comments could shrivel up Yolanda's appetite for days. Another of Jackie's sayings was 'She's let herself go,' delivered with crushing scorn about someone who'd gained a few pounds. So, Yolanda had an ambivalent attitude to food. She loved it, loved cooking it, but feared its power to destroy. At university no one was interested in cooking. Now she had a good salary and worked long hours, picking up a takeaway on her way home had become the norm. Socialising involved drinking rather than eating.

Yolanda and Claudia had planned to eat at local pubs and restaurants, but she didn't fancy walking into unknown pubs on her own. It didn't occur to her that she might cook, she just hoped there were good takeaways nearby. Surely by the seaside there'd be fish and chips. She drove around the corner to the surprisingly varied High Street and easily found a parking space. There was a supermarket where she could buy basics, but next door was a deli – Stefano's. With an attractive window display of home-made pasta, olive oil and artisan bread, this boded well. Inside she found an array of cold meats, cheeses and salads. The shop was empty and the young man behind the counter was happy to discuss and recommend the wares on offer. Yolanda left the shop with the makings of a substantial meal.

Back in the flat, tiredness settled on her shoulders like a blanket. She yawned; it was only six o'clock. Curled up on the sofa, she dozed through several TV programmes. She ate her meal on the balcony in the growing dusk, soaked in a long hot bath and collapsed into the crisp, fresh sheets.

◆ ◆ ◆

Yolanda stretched; she'd slept for twelve hours straight. It must be the sea air, and it'd also given her an appetite. She ate organic muesli on the balcony watching the sea. The weather was as promising as the day before. The sun smiled in an azure sky, and the glistening sea and pale empty beach beckoned.

Yolanda grabbed her sketchbook and crossed the road to the beach. She wandered on the sand, gathering shells and stones, photographing the sea, sky and seaweed clad rocks. She lost track of time. A stream of undemanding images flowed into her brain, leaving no room for deadlines. This was how she felt when she was drawing and painting, a state of flow in which she didn't register any sense of self. It was intoxicating.

On the deserted promenade stood a café, Pav's, a simple one storey building with spotless plastic chairs and tables outside. Yolanda bought a coffee, carried the thick white china cup outside and sat in the sun, her face tilted to its brilliance. An elderly man arrived and sat at the next table. He took out a newspaper, reading as he drank. He looked different from people in London. His face was sunburned, a healthy glow, not from sunbathing, but simply living by the sea.

Yolanda placed the shells and stones she'd gathered on the table, and moved them around, looking for interesting angles, shapes and combinations. She flicked through the photos on her phone. No ideas yet for her drawing. Up till now she had worked in monochrome – black and white and shades of grey, finding abstract patterns and compositions in architecture or the natural world.

She sat back in the chair, her face raised to the sun and her eyes closed. When she opened them, another table was occupied by two elderly ladies who chatted quietly. Had she been sleeping again? There were a couple of walkers on the beach, but the peace, sunshine, expanse of gilded sand and shimmering sea mesmerised her. She felt drugged. More relaxed than she'd thought possible.

After eating poached eggs on toast for lunch at the same table, Yolanda lingered long after she'd finished. At last, she dragged herself up. She couldn't lounge away the day there. She was already horrified at how much time she'd wasted. But was it wasted?

Pockets full of shells and stones, Yolanda strolled back to the flat. She explored her new domain properly, finding a shower room and the second bedroom with twin beds. In this room, French doors led to another balcony. It was the same size as the first, but looked over the back instead of the sea. There was a charming garden below. This balcony was now in full sun. Another place to sit and draw, with quite a different feel. She must get some work done this afternoon, she thought with a stab of guilt. She must have something to show for her time.

Then coming back into the room, she saw it. On the wall, a picture. A portrait. The eyes caught her eyes, and held them fast. A portrait of a woman with long tendrils of hair. The image was stylised, the hair portrayed as a plant growing in all directions, threatening to extend beyond the frame. The colours were unnatural: peach, pale blue, and purple. But the eyes dominated. Yolanda looked into their inky depths, sucked in as if into a deep well. She couldn't draw her own eyes away. The eyes in the picture held her with an irresistible force. Their expression – what was it? Fear, dread, incomprehension, anguish? It was all of these and more.

Her heart beat faster. All the new peace, calm and warm languor seeped away, leaving a raw connection with the face on the wall. The eyes on the wall. Abruptly, she broke the link and lowered her own eyes. She left the room, went into the lounge and sat on the sofa. There were pictures in that room also, but posters. Friendly, light-filled seascapes by Monet. Quite different from the other.

Yolanda had never experienced such a reaction to a picture before. So visceral, intense. The image was burned into her mind, shutting out all else with its throbbing presence. Once more, it drew her back. She stood before the picture and this time looked more closely. It was a painting on canvas, skilfully executed. There was no signature, but the initials, MG, written in small letters in the bottom right-hand corner. She shivered. She couldn't sleep in this room. She shut the door, took her art materials to the other balcony, and sat down to work.

Yolanda arranged a few shells on the small table and began to draw. But as she looked at the images all she could see were faces. Or rather the same face. In the curves of the shells, she saw tendrils of hair curling. From the shadows, eyes challenged her. She pushed the shells aside, looked at the photographs on her phone and found one of a rock pool, surrounded by seaweed covered rocks. She forced herself to draw with her pens, but felt no connection with the composition. It was weak, meaningless – just a series of strokes. Irrelevant.

Her mind returned to the painting in the other room. Who was the subject of the portrait? Who painted it? What did the expression on the sitter's face mean? Yolanda was sure there was a story behind the picture. She must find out what it was.

The ring of the doorbell shocked her, not sure what the noise was. Approaching the front door, she heard a key in the lock.

"Anybody home? It's only me."

Molly came in. "Sorry to disturb you, I've just brought some extra towels. How're you getting on? Anything you need?"

"I'm fine," said Yolanda, "it's a lovely flat." Something occurred to her and she opened the door to the second bedroom. "By the way, that picture, do you know anything about it?"

Molly regarded the painting.

"Not really. I think Marie Claire – that's the owner – when she bought the flat it was here. She lives in London. I think it just came with the flat." She screwed up her face. "Not my sort of thing, not what I'd want in a bedroom. Gives you the creeps."

When Molly had gone, Yolanda returned to her sketchbook and the monochrome drawings. She was seized by a longing for colour that was almost a physical hunger. She put down the grey pen. Senseless, trivial marks. She must have colour. But she'd brought no colour, no pens, pastels, or paint. Claudia was bringing all the coloured media. They agreed it would be foolish to double up, they could share. But Claudia wasn't there. She must be able to buy paints. There must be an art supplies shop around somewhere. But Yolanda was used to London where everything was available. She picked up her phone and googled. Yes, there it was, art supplies – The Paynter's Art – 3.6 miles. Northdown Road, Cliftonville, Margate. Panic over.

Yolanda hopped in the car and followed the satnav instructions. She drove along the main road into Margate, following the curve of the coast past the beach on her left and amusement arcades and cafes on the right. The beach at Margate was much busier and didn't have Westgate's genteel charm. Northdown Road was a surprise, with a strange selection of mostly downmarket shops.

In contrast, The Paynter's Art, had an inviting shop front, with several seascapes displayed in the window as well as enticing (to an artist) materials. Yolanda entered with the excitement of a treasure seeker. The shop was deeper than it appeared. Immediately inside was a display of cards, small paintings and a counter devoted to picture framing. A motherly looking woman stood behind it. She directed Yolanda through an arched doorway into an extensive area containing materials. The range of supplies rivalled any art shop Yolanda had seen in London. She was overwhelmed. Like a child in a sweet shop, she wanted everything. But where to start?

A tall woman finished serving a teenager, and then turned to Yolanda.

"I'm Penny Paynter," smiled the woman, " how can I help you?"

"Is that Paynter, as in the name of the shop?"

"Yes, it's been in my family since 1891. I haven't seen you around before, are you down here on holiday?"

"Yes I suddenly want colour, I've always worked in monochrome. Colour, but nothing that'll make a mess. I'm staying in a rented flat."

Penny considered the matter.

"Also, something portable might be a good idea, that you can take out with you," she said.

Yolanda nodded.

"Watercolour, possibly? said Penny.

"Aren't the colours rather wishy washy?" said Yolanda, "and I'm not keen on brushes, I prefer pens, pastels or pencils. And how do you carry the water around?"

"Watercolour pencils might work; we stock the top brands and the colours are strong. You can use them dry, like a coloured pencil or go over them with water afterwards. We sell these water brushes that have reservoirs to hold water."

Penny showed Yolanda a table with paper and pencils to sample.

"Why don't you have a go, take your time? I'm around if you need me."

Yolanda tried the pencils. Penny was right, the colours were vivid. They were just what she wanted. In the end Yolanda treated herself to a good-sized set of the pencils, and a water brush as well as a new sketchbook. She spent an hour and more money than she intended, but that was invariably the case in an art shop.

"We do mail order," said Penny, as she wrapped up Yolanda's purchases, "so if you need replacements or extra colours – or anything else – just let us know. We're on Instagram if you want to follow us."

Yolanda said nothing. Social media wasn't her thing. She had a few friends on Facebook, but had never been on Instagram.

"We have a gallery upstairs," Penny went on, "you might like to take a look."

Yolanda mounted the stairs hung with more seascapes and local scenes. At the top was a spacious, white walled room with a variety of paintings. As well as the ubiquitous seascapes, there were portraits, florals and abstracts. The standard of the work was generally high. Yolanda examined the paintings, interested to see how the paint was applied. When she came to the far corner, she stopped in her tracks for the second time that day. The painting. It was a highly coloured, stylised portrait. It must be by the same artist as the one in the flat. The one that'd affected her so deeply. Yes, the initials were the same.

Yolanda stood back, her heart beating. A different face. This time an older woman. As before, the artist had focused on the woman's features, especially her eyes. The face was lined with age – the lines like contours on a map. The woman's hair was piled up on her head, revealing dangling earrings in the shape of a sun and a moon. The expression on this sitter's face indicated wisdom and satisfaction. The pronounced lines suggested a life that hadn't always been easy, but one that'd been satisfying. Behind the face, was the shadowy outline of a building, against a dark background, which reinforced the notion of a person in the evening of their life. Yolanda wondered if Penny could give her more information about the artist.

Penny frowned as she considered Yolanda's questions.

"This is an odd one," she said, "the art group had an exhibition here about a year ago. They usually collect any work that isn't sold. I can't remember why they didn't take this."

Seeing Yolanda's disappointment, she went on.

"I can give you the phone number of Wendy who runs the art group. She should be able to help. I've got the number downstairs."

◆ ◆ ◆

Yolanda rang Wendy when she got back to the flat, which she already thought of as home. She explained the situation and Wendy sounded friendly. There was a pause, as if she was trying to recall the picture.

“Yes, I do remember... a portrait, stylised. It wasn't one of our regular members. I think someone brought along a friend or relation – we had room in the exhibition. Her name was Margaret or Margery, something with an M. I'm really sorry I can't be of more help.”

Yolanda thanked Wendy and that seemed to be the end of the conversation.

“Just a minute,” said Wendy, “you said you're down here for a few days, and you're an artist?”

“I wouldn't exactly say I'm an artist, but I like...”

“Anyone who makes art is an artist,” said Wendy, the phrase coming out glibly, as if she'd said it many times before. “If you come along to the art group, you can ask the members yourself.”

“Oh, I don't think...”

“Of course, it's up to you, but we're having our regular meeting tomorrow. Our ‘paint date’ – we have them once a month. We get together, work and have coffee and a chat. Sometimes we have a theme or a still life. If you're not doing anything else, you'd be most welcome.”

Yolanda was silent, which Wendy took for interest.

“Tomorrow it's floral. Of course, you don't have to paint flowers. It’s at Cynthia's house, Kingsgate, near Broadstairs.”

Yolanda surprised herself.

“Well maybe, if you’re sure...”

“The more the merrier. Ten o'clock.”

Wendy proceeded to give Yolanda detailed directions, as if she'd never heard of a satnav.

Yolanda sighed. What'd she let herself in for?

CHAPTER 2

Yolanda hesitated on the doorstep of the chalet bungalow, before ringing the bell. The woman who answered the door looked about the same age as her mum. But there the similarity ended. Cynthia had definitely let herself go, and might even be a housewife, judging by the smell of baking that wafted into the hallway. Another woman of about the same age joined her, and Yolanda's heart sank. Was this a mistake? She noticed a couple of pictures on the wall in the hall. Conventional, amateurish was her instant judgement, however, she was inside now and couldn't leave straightaway. The other woman was Wendy, and she and Cynthia were both warm in their welcome of the newcomer. Steeling herself, Yolanda entered a large sitting room. Yes, most of the people in the room – all women – were at least ten years older than her, but there was one person of her own age.

Everyone introduced themselves, and the younger person turned out to be Robin. Yolanda couldn't help staring. Robin had thick, curly black hair confined by a brightly coloured scarf tied round her head. She wore a tie dyed top and denim jeans exuberantly embroidered. Even her canvas shoes had been decorated with what looked like marker pens.

In the middle of a dining table an arrangement of flowers had been set up. In the adjoining conservatory, were flowers in a bucket, with small vases and other containers for the artists to choose and set up their own subjects. Daunted by the large display, Yolanda chose a single bloom – an orange gerbera – and placed it in a green glass jar. She set the jar on a small table in the conservatory, and took out the shiny flat tin holding her new pencils. She felt self-conscious at first, but seeing the other artists focusing on their own work, realised nobody was looking at her.

Yolanda started by drawing quick sketches of her subject to capture simple shapes. As she grew familiar with the forms of flower and vase, she moved it to capture a variety of compositions. She was in the flow, oblivious to her surroundings.

"Coffee's ready everyone." Cynthia's voice from the sitting room broke in, grounding her in time and space once more. Cynthia came into the conservatory.

"Coffee's ready, Yolanda – or tea if you prefer."

The drinks, in floral china mugs, were in the kitchen, as well as the rock buns and lemon drizzle cake Yolanda had smelled earlier. The artists congregated around the table.

"I suppose there's no point in offering you a cake," said Cynthia to Robin and everyone laughed

"Robin works in the best bakery in town," explained Wendy, "it's called Batchelor's, next door to Paynter's. Have you asked about the painting, Yolanda?"

"No, not yet."

"Listen up everyone," said Wendy, "Yolanda's got something to say."

In a few sentences, Yolanda explained the situation, and showed the photograph she'd taken on her phone of the painting at Paynter's. They all looked, but without much interest. It seemed no one could remember anything.

"You see, we were busy getting our own work ready for the show.

Then there was the private view, and seeing which works sold," said someone else.

"Did you say the name was Margaret?" asked Robin slowly, "I think I remember Gertie bringing her along. She was her cousin or aunt or something."

"Gertie's not here today," said Wendy, "she's in Germany visiting her son. I'll give you her phone number, and you can call her when she gets back next week."

Yolanda didn't feel like phoning another strange person. Anyway, in a few days she'd be back at work, and would've forgotten about the painting. She looked at the others' pictures. There were varying degrees of talent, but most efforts were at best pretty pictures, portraying the floral subjects in a conventional manner. The only person whose work showed real originality, mastery of technique as well as an interesting use of colour, was Robin. The composition, naive style and freshness stood out among the other worthy, but pedestrian pictures. Yolanda wanted to say something to Robin, but found her appearance intimidating. She didn't want to give a trite compliment.

As Yolanda headed back into the conservatory Robin followed her, and looked at the small jar with its single occupant.

"That's a good idea," she said, selected a few flowers and arranged them in a jam jar. She put the arrangement on the floor and sat down beside it. Crossing her legs, she pulled an assortment of marker pens from her pocket, and removed the rubber band holding them together. A small sketchbook came out of another pocket and with quick, decisive strokes, Robin made a picture. It was in no way realistic. Robin had taken elements of the flowers and combined them to form patterns and groups to fill the page. The effect was simple, fresh and harmonious.

"That's amazing," said Yolanda spontaneously. "I really mean it. It's... it gives me a happy feeling." She looked at Robin and they both laughed. Robin stood up and pointed to Yolanda's sketchbook.

"May I?"

Yolanda nodded. "I've just started using colour, I usually work in monochrome," she said.

"This isn't paint, is it? What're you using?" said Robin, flipping through the book.

"I had an urge to work in colour, I bought these yesterday at The Paynter's – at Paynter's." She showed Robin the set of pencils. "You can add water with this," bringing out a water brush.

"Pretty pricey," said Robin taking the tin in her hands and opening it.

"You can use them, if you like," said Yolanda.

"Cheers," said Robin, opening a fresh page in her sketchbook.

They worked in silence. Yolanda stole quick glances at Robin. She was a real artist; she even looked the part, unlike her own sweater in three shades of grey, well-fitting but unremarkable jeans and tan boots.

"Good work, well done all," said Wendy, at the end of the session, "and thanks to Cynthia for the hospitality, the flowers and the cake."

Robin stood up, stashed her pens and sketchbook in her pockets, and slung a small tapestry bag over her shoulder. She and Yolanda were the first to leave, the others packing up slowly and stopping to chat.

"Thanks for the loan of the pencils, Yolanda, nice to meet you," said Robin as they walked down the drive.

"Any time," said Yolanda, but added with a smile, "well not any time actually, I'm only down here for a few days."

Robin looked at her.

"Like to grab a sandwich? There's a pub nearby with a great view.

A bit pricey though."

"Thanks," said Yolanda, "that would be great."

They walked round the cliff and arrived at the Captain Digby, perched on the clifftop, overlooking a sandy bay. Sitting outside in the sunshine, was surreal. Yolanda never made friends as easily as this. She was wary with new people, sizing them up, not revealing too much of herself. She'd watch how they spoke and dressed, to decide whether she wanted to ally herself with them.

This started when she was at school. She was reserved and others didn't know what to make of her. Her mum said, 'Decide which group you want to be in and do what you have to do to fit in.' Yolanda was on the edge of the group of popular girls. She always had cool hairstyles and clothes, which they respected. But not so cool she was a threat to their leadership. It was the same at university. Her mum actually took a day off work to check out the place. Jackie kept her eyes and ears open all day. Then Yolanda was sent off with exactly the right clothes and haircut to fit in with the hard-working ambitious students, the ones her mum wanted her to mix with.

Jackie always had her finger on the pulse of current trends. Each of her salons had a pile of the latest style glossies. Yolanda never saw her reading them, but somehow, she picked up information and could identify the right look for her daughter at every stage of her life.

Jackie's one close friend, George, owned an upmarket clothes shop, 'Georgette', in the smartest part of Leeds. On buying trips, she looked out for suitable items to give Yolanda's wardrobe that extra bit of style. What would Jackie and George make of Robin, Yolanda couldn't help wondering?

Yolanda found Robin open and warm. She spoke freely about herself, without oversharing.

"I got married young," Robin said, "it didn't work out. No kids. Probably just as well. So now I'm staying with my aunt. She's got spare rooms and she likes to have me in the house. Lets me use the attic as a studio and I can borrow the car."

"You work at a bakery?" asked Yolanda, "What was the name?"

"Batchelors. You should try it. It's also a café, an old-fashioned type. Open in the morning but shuts around six. What kind of work do you do?"

"I work in London, in an office."

Yolanda felt uncomfortable saying she was a lawyer, afraid it would make a barrier, affect this possible friendship before it got started.

"I've been going to an art class in London. The idea was to come down here for a few days to get ideas and inspiration for new work. We've got a show coming up. It's only a small thing, but it's my first. I was supposed to come with my friend, it was her idea. But at the last minute she had no one to look after her son. So here I am."

Then the conversation turned to art. They both sat in the sunshine, losing track of time. The sun was surprisingly strong. Robin untied her scarf and ran her fingers through her unruly black hair. She saw Yolanda's surprised look.

"I chop bits off it every so often, but this keeps it out of my face. Never go to hairdresser's – too pricey. Went once and they straightened and coloured it. Never again. Cost an arm and a leg, and it didn't feel like me. Look at the time, I've got to go."

"Of course," said Yolanda standing up, "thanks so much."

◆ ◆ ◆

Back at the flat, Yolanda relaxed. The morning had turned out surprisingly well. Maybe she should forget about the picture in the other room. She opened the door to find out whether it still had the disturbing effect. But once again, looking into the eyes, the expression killed her happy mood, hit her with the same force as before. The room was dark and oppressive. Also, the flat was so quiet, no noise from the neighbours or the road. She found the silence unnerving. She didn't feel like drawing, but decided to get some information about the watercolour pencils she'd bought. There must be YouTube tutorials about them. So, for the next couple of hours, she lost herself down the rabbit hole of the internet, discovering different techniques and effects.

Yolanda yawned. She'd planned to get fish and chips for supper, but couldn't be bothered to go out. She finished the leftovers from the deli and wondered what to do next. As if in answer, her phone rang.

"Hi, Yolanda."

She didn't recognise the voice at first.

"It's me, Robin. I emailed Gertie and she said the name of her friend, the one who painted that picture, is Margery. She hasn't got the contact details with her, but she's flying back tomorrow and she'll be in touch."

"Thanks so much," said Yolanda, "that's really kind of you." Even to her own ears, her voice sounded flat. There was a pause.

"Since you're by yourself," said Robin, "do you want to come to the pub tonight? Meet some of my friends. They're arty, or at least creative types. You'll get on with them."

Yolanda didn't hesitate. Anything to get out of that the lonely, silent flat.

"Yes, I'd really like that. Which pub?"

"The Yard of Ale – it's not far from Paynter's. It's not fancy, but not pricey either. See you later."

◆ ◆ ◆

Yolanda stood in front of the mirror and ran her fingers through her hair, as Robin had done. Her hair was dead straight, smooth as silk. That was what the most up to date, expensive, straightening system promised. Each strand gleamed. It hung – not like silk – more like a high tech, ultra-shiny, perfect new fibre. What was it Robin said about her own hair? 'It didn't feel like me.' Between her fingers Yolanda's hair felt perfectly smooth. But the sheen was synthetic. How would her hair look and feel if it wasn't straightened or coloured, she wondered?

Yolanda considered what to wear. She'd normally change for an evening out, but she didn't want to look overdressed. In the end she just grabbed her tan wool coat and hoped for the best. Hesitating in the doorway of the pub, she spotted Robin who waved. Yolanda took the seat next to her. Robin was wearing the same clothes as earlier, with a shaggy cardigan on top. Jackie wouldn't have used this garment to wash the kitchen floor with. Around the table were four other people. Robin pointed at a guy on her other side.

"Yolanda, this is Andy, he's our tech wizard. And he's writing and illustrating a comic."

"Graphic novel," said Andy, "how many times do I have to tell you, Robin?"

He talked about this project with enthusiasm. Yolanda listened and dredged up from her memory a relevant word.

"Is that manga?" she said doubtfully.

Andy looked at her with interest.

"Yes, totally. I'm heavily influenced by Japanese comic art. You get a real sense of emotion. The Americans draw more realistically and use colour, but there isn't the same depth of feeling. The black and white in manga captures mood." Yolanda watched Andy as he talked earnestly, noticing his receding hairline and faint double chin. 'He's let himself go', would be Jackie's verdict and that would be that.

"Here," said Andy, "look at some of the pages I'm working on now." He pulled up images on his phone and handed it to

Yolanda.

She took it reluctantly, but was shocked. The guy could certainly draw. Marvelling at the strong expressive images, she looked at Andy with new respect.

"These're really powerful," she said, "what's the story?"

"Don't encourage him," groaned Robin, "he'll bend your ear back all night."

"That's okay," said Yolanda, "but can I get you some drinks first?"

"I'll come with you to the bar." said Robin. "Most of us are not flush with cash, so we each buy our own drinks. I'll have a white wine spritzer – heavy on the soda," she told the barman, "This'll last me all night. If I'm really skint I'll just have the soda."

Eyeing the tall glass, Yolanda ordered the same.

Back at the table Robin introduced Tash, Pete and Melody.

"Yolanda's just discovered colour," she said to the group.

Not the sort of conversational gambit Yolanda was used to, but the others leaned forward.

"That's exciting," said Tash, sitting on Yolanda's other side. "Have you been to Canterbury, yet? The cathedral?"

"No, not yet I was planning to go."

"You'll find the stained-glass windows amazing – although I'm biased."

"Tash works in the stained-glass restoration department at the cathedral," said Pete, "it's really worth going. I've got a lot of inspiration there for my work."

Yolanda looked at Pete. He wore a flat tweed cap, checked shirt and loose-fitting corduroy waistcoat. He had a sparse, sandy beard and looked like her idea of a folk singer. Pete's unconventional clothes gave the impression he was an 'eccentric', and wanted to attract attention. However, under the hat brim, his fine-featured face looked sensitive and reserved.

An interesting combination. Yolanda was intrigued.

"Pete's a jewellery designer," said Tash, "these're his." She pointed to the translucent triangles with delicate flashes of colour, hanging from her ears. "I work with colour so much, I like to wear neutrals, but these're subtle. Seriously, if you come to the cathedral, give me a call and I'll show you around the workshop."

"Thanks. How did you get into that kind of work?" Yolanda asked.

"I studied art and then got interested in stained glass. I did internships in France and Herefordshire and then got certified. I started working at the cathedral three years ago, it's my dream job." Tash went on, "Isn't Robin great? How did you meet her?"

"At the art group – she befriended me – all the others were my mum's age. She's really talented," Yolanda said.

"She befriended me too. When I found a flat near here, I went into Batchelor's a couple of times and got talking to her. She heard I was moving and brought Andy along to help."

After that, the conversation turned to local matters that Yolanda knew nothing about. She sat back and watched the others talk. When Andy made a joke, Pete who'd been serious before, smiled. His whole face brightened and the features softened. His eyes met hers and the smile vanished. He looked down. This man was no show off, whatever his clothes indicated. Yolanda found her gaze returning to Pete's face for another glimpse of that gentle smile.

They were the most creative and welcoming bunch she'd ever met. They took her at face value. But as the evening went on, Yolanda revised her opinion. Melody wasn't so friendly. She glanced several times at Yolanda, taking in her hair, makeup and generally sizing her up. Melody was wearing what Jackie would dismissively call, 'chain store clothes'. Superficially these were similar to Yolanda's, but of inferior quality of both fabric and style. She hoped Melody wasn't jealous. 'Jealousy's a compliment, but it makes enemies', was another of Jackie's sayings. With this in mind, Yolanda made an effort to be friendly, asking Melody where she lived and other commonplace questions. The answers were monosyllabic.

Robin looked down at her phone.

"Hey, Yolanda, Gertie's just emailed me to say she's come across Margery's contact details. She says she hasn't heard from her for ages, it seems they aren't close. I'll send it on to you."

"Thanks so much," said Yolanda.

Just before eleven, Robin stood up.

"I'll be off now," she said yawning.

That broke up the evening, and everyone else got ready to leave as well.

"Nice to meet you, Yolanda," said Tash and Andy and Pete nodded.

"We're here most weeknights," said Robin, "pop in if you're free." As they walked out together, she went on, "let me know what happens with Margery."

◆ ◆ ◆

Sipping tea on the sofa in the flat, Yolanda reflected on the evening. It was quite different from her usual drinks get togethers. Her group of 'friends', mostly from work, dressed up and met in an upmarket bar or nightclub. Yolanda would spend the night balancing her intake of cocktails and shots to keep up with the others, but not drinking so much she lost control. A task that wasn't easy. Conversation was aimed at making others aware of the speaker's own success and achievements, while mercilessly slagging off targets outside the chosen group, and spending a fortune. What a difference this evening had been in every way. How she'd enjoyed it. The white wine spritzer was refreshing, and her head was still clear. She checked the information Robin had sent about Margery. There was a phone number and also an address in a place called Tankerton. She'd call tomorrow.

◆ ◆ ◆

Miraculously the good weather continued. In the morning, Yolanda remembered the mention of Canterbury Cathedral and decided to go there. She found a car park at the edge of the city, and walked to the cathedral along quaint streets lined with independent shops, galleries and cafes. She stopped for a coffee at a vegetarian cafe, where the brightly coloured decor reminded her of Robin. Yolanda considered phoning Tash, as the latter had suggested yesterday, but this wasn't the way she usually did things. She hardly knew Tash. Maybe Tash was being polite, she might be busy. But mostly it was Yolanda's protective armour that dissuaded her from this course of action. Instead, she rang the number for Margery. The sound of the tone wasn't the usual one, and there was no reply.

◆ ◆ ◆

Yolanda's idea of stained glass was the memory of a church she'd visited as a child. She entered the cathedral expecting to be impressed. What she didn't expect was to be transported into another dimension. Nothing could've prepared her for the age, majesty and sheer beauty of the cathedral. The stained-glass windows, their colours heightened by the brilliant sunshine, appeared to be constructed of living gemstones. Molten emeralds, rubies and sapphires formed a patchwork of pure colour.

The concentrated beams of variegated light pierced Yolanda's soul. Her reaction to the haunting portrait that hung in the flat, had unlocked a channel to the heart she'd protected for so many years. The layers of control she'd built up against real or perceived attacks, had shielded her, but at the same time formed a barrier disabling her emotions. She wanted colour – and here was colour in its purest form. She drank in the varied hues without even seeing the images. Time swiftly passed as she moved from one window to another in a daze, feeling the giddiness that hadn't followed her evening in the pub.

Lightheaded, Yolanda finally wandered outside, blinking in the strong sunlight, wondering what to do next. In front of her was the cathedral shop and she went in. Immediately a book on the history of stained glass caught her eye. It was a huge coffee table tome, and the illustrations were gorgeous. Without checking the price, and nearly collapsing under the weight, Yolanda carried it to the cashier. The price was high, but she'd normally have spent a similar sum on drinks the night before.

Yolanda sat in the sun, eating a ploughman's lunch. She tried phoning Margery again. Still the same strange sound. Sitting back with the glorious sun warming her face, fear of the picture at the flat waned. Interest grew stronger. On an impulse, she checked how far Tankerton was. Twenty minutes. She could go there on her way home.

◆ ◆ ◆

As she walked to the car, her phone rang. It was Jackie.

"George is coming up to London tomorrow, she wants to use the flat for a few days," Jackie said after the usual greetings.

This wasn't an uncommon request. On her buying trips to London, George often slept on Yolanda's sofa bed.

"Yes, er..."

"What's the matter?"

"I'm actually away for a few days."

"Where?"

"East Kent. The coast, near Canterbury."

"What're you doing there? Business?"

"Not exactly..."

"Is it a man? You don't want to start... you've got lots of time."

"It's not a man."

"You need to establish your career, don't tie yourself down to some man at this stage."

"Actually, I'm having meetings down here. With local – suppliers, creators."

"Why've they sent you down there? You want to be careful. Don't let them side-line you. There's no future in that area. I told you, you've got to show you're indispensable. Needed. In London."

"Yes Mum, but it's not like that..."

"Well, can George stay in the flat?"

"Of course."

"Yolanda don't take your eye off the ball. You've got to know where you're heading and go all out for it. Otherwise, someone else will walk all over you and get there first. I've told you before, you can't stand still in life. You're either on your way up or down."

"Yes, Mum."

Yolanda sighed. Her mother was relentless. Exhausting. There were good reasons for her attitude to life, money and men, but Jackie never entertained the possibility that her daughter could have any other goals than her own. Yolanda knew that up to now, she'd been living her life according to her mum's ideas and aspirations. It was simpler that way.

◆ ◆ ◆

Arriving outside twelve, Wardown Road, Tankerton, Yolanda noticed a car in the drive. Somebody must be home. She tried the phone number again. No connection. She got out of the car, took a deep breath and pressed the doorbell.

It was opened by a man in his fifties.

“Hello, I'm looking for Margery Gresham,” Yolanda said, “I got her contact details from Gertie...,” she realised she didn't know Gertie’s surname, “the art group in Margate.”

The man looked at her.

“I did try and call, but her phone doesn't seem to be working.”

He continued to stare at Yolanda as if he didn't understand her words. Finally, he spoke.

“My mother passed away.”

CHAPTER 3

"Oh no. I'm so sorry, I didn't mean to intrude." Yolanda turned to go.

"No," said the man, "it was a while ago. It's okay. What did you want?"

"I don't want to bother you, but it's about your mum's paintings. I've seen two of them. I wanted to find out more about them. They weren't signed, only initials, but I found out about your mum through the art group."

"Please come in," he said, "I'm John."

"If you're sure, I'm Yolanda Blake." He nodded and she followed him inside.

One of Margery's paintings hung in the hall. Another portrait in her distinctive style. Yolanda stopped in front of it.

"You recognise it?" said John, "there're others inside."

In the living room there were two more of Margery's portraits, both arresting, but neither gave Yolanda the visceral feeling she experienced with the one in the flat. They sat down.

"What did you want to know?" John asked.

"Your mum's work's amazing, and so original. I'd like to know about the subject of her portraits. Do you know who the people are in the pictures?"

John thought for a moment, then stood up.

"Hang on a minute." He left the room and Yolanda heard him go up the stairs.

He returned carrying a large cardboard box, which he set down on the floor. It was full of newspapers. John took out the top one.

"*East Kent Gazette*," he said, "my mother used photographs from the paper for her pictures. My father hoarded newspapers in the attic. She hated it, was always on at him about it. But when he died, she couldn't bring herself to throw out the old papers. My mother only took up painting when she retired. All her paintings were based on photographs from the *East Kent Gazette*."

He paused. "Did you say you were an artist?"

"Yes, sort of, in a small way."

"You can have these," John pointed to the box of newspapers, "they're no good to me. I should've thrown them out. You'd be doing me a favour if you took them."

"If you say so. Thanks very much."

John picked up the box, "Shall I give you a hand? Do you have a car?"

"My car's outside, but I can manage, thanks." She took the box from him.

He escorted her into the hall and opened the front door. Yolanda hesitated.

"Your mother was a talented artist; her work is powerful."

He smiled. "Thanks. I thought it was good, and she sold some pictures. It's nice to know other people appreciated her work. Good luck, I hope you find what you're looking for."

◆ ◆ ◆

Yolanda carried the box of newspapers up to the flat and put it on the dining table. She'd look at them later, she needed space first. Sitting on the sofa with a cup of tea, she thought of Robin. She must tell her what'd happened. It was after six, Robin would've finished work.

"Hi, it's Yolanda, I've got some news,"

"Hi, sorry I can't speak at the moment. Are you coming to the pub tonight, we can talk there?"

"Sure, see you later."

Why not? She'd time to relax first and grab a bite to eat. Yolanda remembered the book on stained glass and brought it in from the car. She curled up on the sofa, skimming through the pictures. Something was distracting her, and she put down the book with an impatient gesture. She looked over at the box of newspapers. It stood there, on the table, brimming over with possibility.

Sitting at the table, Yolanda took out the top newspaper. It was brittle with age. The date was 1999. She unfolded the paper carefully. On the front page a rectangular piece had been cut out, between the main headline and the article below. The missing piece must be a photograph. She read the headline 'Treasure trove of Roman coins found in field.' She looked down to the article, which was about a farmer, who'd discovered a cache of silver Roman coins with a metal detector.

Did Margery cut out the photograph to use as a reference image for her painting? Yolanda placed the paper on the table and took another from the box. This time the front page was intact. She turned the pages carefully. In the middle there was another neatly cut out space. The caption was 'Master of horror cinema dies.' Half the page was devoted to one subject. It described the death of someone called Peter Cushing who'd lived in Whitstable. There were several photographs of the actor in different roles. One was missing. Presumably, Margery chose this as another starting point for a picture. Yolanda checked all the newspapers in the box. There were twenty-five in total and every one had a picture cut out. So, they wouldn't reveal the information she wanted. It was a blow.

◆ ◆ ◆

The same group gathered in the pub, apart from Tash, and they greeted Yolanda like an old friend. All except Melody who merely nodded. Robin turned to Pete.

“Hey, did you bring that necklace – the one for my aunt?”

“Oh no, Robin, I forgot. I'm so sorry – I really am. I know you wanted to give it to her for the weekend. Can I bring it round to the shop tomorrow?”

“No problem. Bring it anytime. You're giving me such a big discount, I can't expect –”

“That's got nothing to do with it. That's no excuse. Thanks for being so understanding. I'll bring it tomorrow, as early as I can. I'm so sorry.”

Melody watched Pete for a while. He noticed her look.

“What's the matter?”

“I've never heard a man apologise so well before, in fact, I've rarely known a man to apologise at all.” Pete frowned. His lips were set in a hard line. He looked down at the table without speaking. Something about Melody’s remarks bothered him, but Yolanda had no idea what.

“I thought women liked men to be strong and silent,” said Andy, “masterful.”

“You're not any of those – so you've got no hope,” said Robin. “I'll never let a man control me again.” she added quietly with unusual bitterness.

“Women can be just as controlling,” Yolanda said, thinking of Jackie.

“I can't imagine anyone controlling you,” said Pete, “You’re too confident. Independent.”

Yolanda coloured.

"I'm working on it."

At the bar Yolanda told Robin about the old newspapers.

"What a shame, but maybe you can get hold of back issues of the paper? If you have the dates."

"That's true." Yolanda hadn't had time to think this out.

"Has anybody got old copies of the *East Kent Gazette*?" asked Robin when they were back at the table. The others shook their heads.

"You should be able to search the archive online," said Andy, "Melody, what do you think?"

"There's a database online, the British Newspaper Archive. You need a subscription though."

"Melody works at the university library, in Canterbury," said Andy.

Melody's expression plainly showed she wasn't willing to help.

"Let me see," said Andy, looking at his phone. "Here, I've found it – the *East Kent Gazette* office, it's in Deal. You could try them."

"Thanks very much."

"I'll send you the info," he said.

Yolanda sipped her drink. So, there was hope after all.

"How's the graphic novel going?" she asked Andy, and he proceeded to tell her.

"Where's Tash?" she asked when he'd finished.

"She has choir on Thursday night."

The others talked about a gig they were going to on Saturday night. Folk music. It seemed there was a folk club in a pub in Broadstairs.

"I won't be here tomorrow night," said Robin, "my aunt's going away and she wants me to help her get ready."

"But you're coming to the gig?" asked Andy.

"Yes."

"Let me know if you need a lift," he said.

Yolanda sat back for the rest of the evening, happy to be with people. It was nice not to have to make an effort.

"By the way, Yolanda, did you want to see my work?" Robin said.

"Of course."

"If you're free, I'm on the early shift on Saturday, do you want to come over? I'll bring some leftovers from the bakery."

"I'd love to, what time?"

"Come about four. This is the address, it's just round the corner from here. See you then."

Pete grinned at Yolanda.

"Are you coming tomorrow night? We'll still be here."

She smiled back.

"Thanks."

Melody looked at Yolanda.

"I see you've made another conquest," she said quietly, her words emerging as a hiss. Only Pete heard, and he started, jerking backwards in his chair. Yolanda raised her eyebrows.

Back at the flat, she couldn't resist the box of newspapers. Robin was right, if she could see the archives for those dates, she'd find the picture she was looking for. But more than that, the articles might contain clues, so she could rule out some of the issues. The picture wasn't of a man, so she could rule out the articles about men.

Although it was late, she sorted the papers. She made two piles, female and male. Ten of the twenty-five articles were about women. Now, her eyes were closing and she went to bed.

◆ ◆ ◆

In spite of her late night, Yolanda woke up early. She ate her muesli on the balcony and showered, but it was still too early to phone the newspaper office. She took the pile of newspapers with missing pictures of stories about women, and made a list of the dates. Then she read the articles. The first one was about a young local athlete, a female swimmer, who'd been selected for the Olympics. That didn't sound like the right one, she would look happy and triumphant. The next one was about a woman in her forties who, as the headlines said had been, "Betrayed by a serial bigamist." That could explain the anxious expression.

Yolanda couldn't wait any longer, surely the newspaper office must be open by now. The phone was answered by a pleasant female voice. Yes, they did keep back issues of the newspaper on microfiche. Yolanda was welcome to come in and the speaker would help her.

"If you want to come in today, I'm here till twelve thirty," said the helpful woman.

Yolanda jumped in the car. The traffic was heavier than she expected, and she was caught in the tail end of the rush hour, but it was still a pleasant drive. The road followed the coast.

The helpful woman was just as friendly in person as over the phone. She left her desk at the reception, and led Yolanda to a small room at the back. There was a table with a kettle and mugs as well as a desk with the microfiche reader. Yolanda explained the particular newspaper issues she wanted to view, and the woman showed her how to use the system. It was straightforward and intuitive, and Yolanda was soon scrolling through past issues. She started with the most recent, which were still six years old.

Her heart thudding, she brought up on the screen and saw for the first time, the picture of the woman betrayed by the serial bigamist. This wasn't the image in the portrait. Even though that was significantly stylised, this photograph was shot from a different angle, and the direction of the subject's gaze wasn't right. Yolanda scrutinised the image carefully. No, it was impossible. Crossing it off her list, she went on to the next one.

Then came a photograph of a woman who'd been accused of killing her lover. Again, Yolanda's heart beat faster as the image appeared. That situation could explain the complex, disturbing expression in the portrait. But no, Yolanda exhaled, not realising she'd been holding her breath. This wasn't the right one either.

For the next half an hour, she systematically trawled through the list. An Olympic athlete, a girl injured in a car crash, a retired headmistress and a young woman who'd carried out a clever fraud all paraded before Yolanda's searching gaze. Then doubt crept in. Was this a waste of time? Maybe Margery had taken her reference from a different source. But she must continue.

She scrolled to the next issue and there it was. The same camera shot, the same shaped face and the same expression in the eyes. Yolanda understood why Margery had chosen this image. It was more disturbing and compelling than any of the others. The quality was poor, a photograph reprinted in a newspaper ten years ago was unlikely to be of high quality. But Yolanda could see enough. The picture wasn't posed, but a snapshot capturing an expression of someone unaware they were being photographed. Even the grainy finish couldn't hide the complex, raw emotion in the subject's eyes.

Margery had painted massed tendrils of hair, curling around the face of the girl and almost filling the canvas. In the photograph also, the long, thick curly hair had a life of its own. A small face peered out between two masses of hair, neither dark nor light. As in the portrait, the eyes dominated. The hair covered part of the face, as if the girl was peering out between two heavy curtains.

But who was the girl? Yolanda dragged her gaze away from the photograph and read the headline, 'Girl goes missing at Folk Week, police suspect foul play.' She read the article.

Beth Winthrop, 23, of Chelmsford, went missing four days ago during the annual Folk Week held at Broadstairs.

Beth was last seen by her friend Amber, with whom she attended the event. Beth left the tent where the girls were camping, saying she was going to attend a performance by a folk singer.

Beth's parents, Linda and Phillip Winthrop, became alarmed when she didn't return home as expected. Hundreds of music fans descend on Broadstairs during Folk Week, the busiest time of the year.

DCI Tom Strachan, who is leading the inquiry, said the police are taking Beth's disappearance very seriously, and foul play has not been ruled out.

Anyone who has seen Beth or has any knowledge of her whereabouts should contact...

She had found out what she wanted. Now she needed a copy of the photograph. Once again help was available. The photo could be enlarged, but this would affect the already poor quality. A compromise was reached and her kind friend pressed the button.

"What's that?" said a woman's voice, peering over Yolanda's shoulder, "Oh yes, that's one of mine."

The speaker had well-cut grey hair and red framed glasses. She smiled and pointed at the screen.

"That's me, Fearne O'Keeffe. I wrote the article. Would you believe I'm still here, that must be ten years ago?"

"I've been trying to find out about this story," said Yolanda, "do you know any more than is in the article?"

"Well now, let me think, it was a long time ago. Yes, I remember there were some odd points about the case."

She looked at her watch.

"If you want, we could get a coffee..."

Yolanda glanced towards the kettle.

"No, none of that stuff, a proper cup of coffee. There's a place down the road."

"Thanks very much. I'd like to find out anything you can tell me."

They were soon sitting in a small cafe with cups of excellent coffee in front of them.

"How come you're so interested in this case?" asked Fearne.

Yolanda told her the whole story.

"I've never been affected like that by a picture. In fact, I'm a logical, unemotional person. It's not like me. That's why it's so strange. It's the expression on her face, the look in her eyes. I feel I must find out what it is and what caused it."

She showed Fearne the photograph.

"Yes, I know what you mean. It's one of the strange things, that photo was supplied by Beth's parents. The only one. I was well in with the police, so I knew all about it. Don't you think most parents of a twenty-three-year-old girl would have better photos than that? It's not the one most parents would choose, and why weren't there any others?"

Yolanda considered this in silence.

"And the other thing is, nobody reported Beth's disappearance until after the Folk Week had finished. If Beth was with her friend, and disappeared while they were there, why didn't the friend report her missing straightaway?"

"That's even more surprising," said Yolanda, "did you find out why?"

Fearne screwed up her eyes.

"Yes, it's coming back to me. What was the friend's name?"

"Amber."

"That's right. Well, the police questioned her, and it turned out they weren't such good friends. The girls had been to the same school, but they hardly knew each other. It wasn't clear why they'd go on holiday together. Amber said she thought Beth had met someone – a man – and gone off with him. But it sounded odd."

"What did the police think?"

"There was someone they were interested in, a suspect. He was the singer mentioned in the article. They questioned him, but in the end, there was no evidence and they had to let him go."

"What did they think?"

"Maybe he killed Beth and hid her body. Maybe he was the man she met and they had a row."

"Do you know his name?" Yolanda asked.

"I can't remember, but I could probably find out. Give me your phone number and I'll let you know."

"What happened in the end? Did Beth turn up?"

"As far as I know, the case was never solved. Beth never turned up and no body was found. Mind you it would be easy enough for her to have gone over the Channel to France. In the end, that's what the police decided must've happened. She met someone and went off abroad with him. That's the last I heard about it."

Fearne finished her coffee.

"I've got to go. It's been nice talking to you, I hope it was helpful."

"Yes, thanks very much. It's been good to hear about it from the horse's mouth as it were. Thanks for taking the time."

"No problem. If I find out that guy's name, I'll send it to you. Here's my card. Let me know if you find out anything interesting, I wouldn't mind doing a follow up article."

Yolanda had a lot to think about. It was a piece of luck that Fearne still worked at the paper after all those years. Now she knew about Beth and her story, she wanted to find out more about the Folk Week and the man the police suspected.

◆ ◆ ◆

While Yolanda was away, she didn't want to receive a constant barrage of emails from her office. So, she set up an automated reply to her office email and checked her account regularly, in case anything important cropped up. She was stunned to read an email from the office. It was about the big case she was working on. An important client and a lot of money was riding on the outcome, and they were due to go to trial the following week. The email, couched in excited terms for a law firm, celebrated the fact that contrary to expectations, the case had been settled out of court. A good result for their client and payment of their legal fees, without the uncertainty of a trial. Her department was planning a big celebration.

Yolanda stared at the email, thinking of its effect on her work. Instead of a stressful trial with long hours for the next couple of weeks, her diary was now empty for that period. Of course, there was other work she could do. While she was thinking about this, her phone rang, it was Molly.

“Hi, how's everything going? Are you having a good time? You've certainly been lucky with the weather. I've got a message from Marie Claire – you know the owner of the flat. The people coming in after you have cancelled, so she said if you wanted to stay another week, you can have the flat at a lower rate. I’ll come in and clean and change the bedding and towels. What do you think?”

The combination of this and the email from her office, made Yolanda think. It was possible.

“I might be interested,” she told Molly, “I'll have to check with work. I'll get back to you as soon as I can.”

She really could stay on at the flat for another week if she wanted to. But did she want to? The trip hadn’t turned out as expected. It wasn't great being alone in the flat. But on the other hand, she’d met Robin and the others. She was having new experiences, and Robin could become a good friend. And there was the picture.

She went into the other room and looked at it again. She

shivered. The face, the expression was even more compelling than before. She stared into those eyes, drawn towards them. Her heart quivered as if it'd been squeezed. Now she knew Beth's name and about her disappearance, she had to find out the answers. And she could only do it here. She'd stay another week.

Yolanda had plenty of leave left, she never took her full allowance, but technically she needed to get permission from her team leader, Gareth. She sent him a quick email, requesting another week off. A few minutes later her phone rang. It wasn't Gareth, but Harvey, another member of the team.

"Hi Yolanda, Harvey here. I've got your email in front of me. Gareth is very busy at the moment – wall to wall meetings – and he's asked me to take over some admin."

"Hi Harvey, great news about the settlement."

Harvey ignored the comment.

"I see you want to take next week off, but aren't you on leave at the moment?"

"Yes, but I've got leave owing to me. And with the case settling –"

"So, you're saying you want to take two weeks off in a row? That's rather unusual, are there any special circumstances?"

Yolanda was fuming. Harvey had no authority over her, whatever he said. He was just being bloody-minded – making her life difficult. He always reminded her of a book she'd read, '*The Arrogance of the Alpha Male*'. There were plenty of those in the firm, and quite a few alpha females as well.

"I have leave available, and nothing in the diary for next week, what's the problem?"

"No problem, but it's not usual to take two weeks off in a row, it sets a precedent."

"I don't understand what you're getting at."

He tried a different approach.

"So, you're saying you're not needed in the office for a fortnight? Is that wise? Some people, like Gareth, for instance, might get the idea you're dispensable. I wouldn't like to take a chance like that. But it's up to you."

Yolanda ended the call. Harvey was quite likely to run to Gareth, putting the worst spin on her request. She thought for a while and then rang another number at the firm.

"Hi Rob, it's Yolanda. Great news about the settlement, isn't it? Yes thanks, but it's the whole team, kudos all round. Listen. With the case settling early, I thought I'd take another week's leave – nobody else goes away now – it's not the school holidays. I don't want to bother Gareth, wall to wall meetings, you know. Could you clear it with him for me? And send me an email to confirm? Thanks, I owe you a drink."

◆ ◆ ◆

Yolanda realised that if she was staying another week, she'd need more shopping. She nipped down to the High Street, but Friday afternoon was busy and the parking space she found was halfway back to the flat. Walking along the High Street, she noticed the range of shops with interest. Stopping outside a butcher, she looked at the steaks. Without the pressure of work, she had time to cook.

There were two estate agents on the High Street and she studied the properties for sale in the window. One flat caught her eye and she examined the photographs of the interior. It must be in the same block as the one she was staying in. Then she saw the price. It was considerably lower than that of her smaller, one-bedroom flat in London. It would be cheaper to live down here. Unconsciously she filed away the idea.

In Stefano's, she bought salads. She must take something to Robin tomorrow, she'd been so kind. Yolanda hesitated between wine and cider. Neither seemed right. Then she spotted a flower shop. The colourful array in the window, made Yolanda think of Robin. She came out of the shop with a multi-coloured bunch for Robin and a smaller one for herself.

Back at the flat, she found a vase and put her flowers on the dining table. She took out her sketchbook and pencils and sat down to draw the arrangement. At first, she drew carefully, trying to reproduce the shapes, colours and arrangement. But then she turned the page and started again, using freer strokes. She worked faster, looking at the flowers rather than the page, losing herself in the work. She filled more and more pages, using large, loose strokes, capturing how the flowers made her feel rather than the blooms themselves.

As the light began to fail, Yolanda looked up. How long had she been working? Grilling the steak, the first cooking she'd done in the flat, she felt at home. Would she really like to live there?

CHAPTER 4

Yolanda regarded her clothes with a sigh. Everything looked drab and dull – she had a sudden feeling of revulsion for the grey, beige and black of her wardrobe. As a young teenager, she'd made a couple of disastrous fashion choices – at least Jackie said they were disastrous. After that, all her clothes were chosen and supplied by George, and Jackie selected her hairstyle. For years, she'd accepted this arrangement – her image was in safe hands. She heard admiring comments from women in the office when they thought she wasn't listening.
"Yolanda's got amazing style," said one, "she never puts a foot wrong, always on trend, but not extreme."

"Impeccable taste," said the other, "and that hair – like a mirror. She never has a bad hair day. I'd kill for hair like that."

The style was impeccable, but for the first time Yolanda wondered, was it her style?

As in her artwork, she was hungry for colour. She didn't expect to stay a fortnight, and hadn't brought enough clothes, she'd have to buy something. Acting on impulse was alien to her. Everything she did was in accordance with the bigger plan. Her mum's plan, she realised. Any spontaneity she possessed, had been repressed or ignored, but not wholly eradicated, it would seem. Rushing out to buy a set of pencils or sweater on a whim, was a minor act, but even this gave her a thrill of freedom. Was this a tear in the cocoon that surrounded her?

Where to go? Google came up with a couple of independent shops in Margate Old Town. In contrast to the garish, downmarket seafront, this area had been gentrified. Bistro tables spilled into a small pedestrianised square with an urban village vibe. 'Pearl Grey' looked promising and Yolanda went in.

She checked the rails of dresses, but they were either too formal or too grungy. A deceptively simple cotton sweater draped across a shelf caught her eye. On the shelf below lay a rainbow pile of the same garments. Yolanda discounted the black, grey, and navy. There was also dusky pink, denim blue and bottle green. But her gaze went straight to a soft turquoise. She unfolded the sweater and examined it. The finish and design would've met George and Jackie's exacting standards, but the colour wouldn't.

The assistant came over.

"Gorgeous colour, isn't it? Would you like to try it on?"

The sweater made Yolanda think of sea and sunshine mixed together. She didn't want to take it off. Without hesitation she paid and instructed the girl to place her own grey sweater in a bag. Coming out of the shop, she couldn't help touching the soft cotton and looking down at her arms encased in that delicious colour. Spirits soaring, she walked into the sunshine.

She wandered around the Old Town, noting the quirky shops and cafes for future visits. Walking towards the sea, she saw a sign for the Turner Contemporary Art Centre. Although she'd lived in London for years, Yolanda had never visited a gallery or art museum until she started her art class. But the teacher encouraged all the students to take advantage of the city's wonderful art resources and she was hooked.

She made for the Turner Centre – a small modern building located next to the sea – and entered the lobby, looking around to see what was going on.

"Yolanda," a voice called, "over here."

Pete smiled and waved. He was wearing a hat as usual – a grey pork pie, corduroy waistcoat and denim shirt.

"Are you going to the exhibition?" he asked.

"I'm not sure, what about you?"

"I'm here delivering stock. The gift shop sells my pieces. But I've seen the exhibition. It's interesting. Food for the creative soul." he announced as if quoting. They both laughed.

"Are you coming to the gig tonight?" he asked.

"I don't know."

"You should come, it'll be good. The Bradstow Mill in Broadstairs. It starts at eight thirty."

"I might."

"Anyway, I've got some more deliveries," said Pete, "good to see you, have a nice day."

Yolanda took his advice and wandered around the small exhibition. She'd never heard of the artist, a local man, but she found the work intriguing. The pieces were all abstract, mostly in shades of black, grey and white, but each had a small, arresting area of vivid colour, which attracted the eye. The one that particularly appealed to her had an area of light blue green. She stood in front of the painting for a while. Her eyes moved from the sombre dark grey and black to the bright colour and back again, as if sensing a dialogue between the two.

In the gift shop, Yolanda looked out for Pete's jewellery, and there it was in a glass case, delicate slivers of colour suspended in transparent shapes. She must ask him how he made them. Then she saw merchandise related to the current exhibition, the one she'd just seen. There was a catalogue for sale, and posters as well as mugs. But what caught her eye was a tote bag decorated with the image of the painting she preferred. She picked up the bag. Her sketchbook would fit – she could use it to carry her art materials. At the cash desk, the girl with pink hair and tattoos covering her bare arms, commented.

“Nice colour, matches your jumper.”

And of course, it did. The blue green on the image was almost exactly the same shade as her new sweater.

Just after four, Yolanda drove up to Robin’s place, a large, solid, period house. Carrying the bouquet of flowers, she rang the doorbell. Robin opened the door wearing a white tunic with multicoloured embroidery, red jeans and a blue scarf around her head.

“Wow, these’re gorgeous. They must’ve been pricey.”

Yolanda smiled and followed her friend inside. In the spacious old-fashioned kitchen, Robin found a large white vase. The flowers did look magnificent.

“The kettle’s on, are you ready for a cuppa?” She opened paper bags and put scones, doughnuts and sausage rolls on a plate. Even though not absolutely fresh, the food was delicious.

“I really must come to the bakery,” Yolanda said.

“Yes, it's quite special. The owner learned to bake from a Swiss guy, and everything is top class. We do special cakes and desserts for parties.

How's the search going, any luck at *The Gazette* office?”

“Yes,” said Yolanda, and she told Robin everything that had happened. Robin stared at the photo and read the newspaper article.

“Sounds like you did a pretty good job. Lucky that journalist was still there. What’re you going to do now? Is that it, now you know the story?”

“In a way, I've got more questions than before, I want to know more about Beth and what happened to her.

”How much time do you have, I thought you were going back to

London?"

"Actually, I'm staying longer," said Yolanda and explained the combination of events.

Robin's face lit up.

"Another week, I'm so glad. The others will be pleased."

Apart from Melody, Yolanda thought but didn't say.

"That's a cool sweater," said Robin, "the colour suits you – you look more alive."

"Where do you get your clothes from, they're unique?" Yolanda had been dying to ask the question.

Robin grinned.

"Charity shops."

Yolanda couldn't hide her surprise and distaste.

"They're great, if you know where to go. When I came down here and met Pete, he put me onto it. He gets all his clothes and hats in charity shops. If you're interested, he'll give you some tips. Come and have a look at my clothes, most of them are from charity shops."

She took Yolanda to her bedroom and opened a wardrobe crammed with her finds.

"These're all one offs; you'll never see anyone else wearing the same thing. Here, try this scarf, it goes with your sweater."

She brought out a fringed scarf made of silky yarn. There were swirls of yellow, green, turquoise and white. She wound it round Yolanda's neck and pointed to a mirror. Yolanda looked at herself, and caught her breath. The face that looked back at her was lightly tanned, and the bright colours of the scarf enhanced the effect. Her hair had lost its glassy sheen, and the ends were beginning to curl. This would normally trigger an urgent call to the only hairdressing salon in London Jackie trusted. But for the first time, Yolanda rebelled. She did look more alive.

"That scarf suits you, keep it, I've got loads more."

Yolanda studied her reflection.

"By the way, are Andy or Pete – seeing anyone? Do you know?" she said trying to sound casual.

Robin looked at her sharply.

"Andy?"

"Well, actually Pete."

Robin untied her headscarf, ran her fingers through her hair and retied it. She looked at Yolanda.

"Not as far as I know. But he's a private person. He's in the pub with us most nights, but..."

There was something she wasn't saying, but Yolanda didn't push her.

◆ ◆ ◆

After this, they went up to the attic which Robin used as a studio. The space was full of her bright, cheerful, deceptively simple canvases of all sizes. The effect was like walking in a summer meadow. They talked art for a while, then Yolanda noticed the time.

"I'd better be going."

"I hoped you'd come to the gig tonight, but if you can't..."

"I'd like to come, shall I drive?"

"Would you mind? My aunt's taken her car."

They arrived at the pub in Broadstairs to find Pete and Melody sitting at a table. Melody took in their arrival together, and the scarf round Yolanda's neck.

"You two look cosy," she said wryly.

Pete, on the other hand, grinned at Yolanda.

"I'm glad you decided to come." He pulled out the chair next to him. "Great scarf. I noticed the sweater this morning. It suits you."

Yolanda smiled, but when she looked into his eyes, she saw a flash of something deeper than the simple words conveyed. An emotion stronger than mere flirtation.

Soon Tash and Andy arrived. He was wearing a sweatshirt with the words, 'Not all who wander are lost', on the front.

"Isn't that a quotation?" said Yolanda.

"Yes, from my favourite book –"

"*Lord of the Rings*," said Pete and Tash together.

"I found it this week in a charity shop. It was as good as new," Andy said. "I'd never have worn second hand clothes before I met you lot, but now I don't like buying new – it seems a waste of money."

"I like to have unusual clothes, but I can't afford much on my wages," Robin said.

"There's a website where you can get all kinds of tips about how to save money. Special deals and cool ideas." said Andy, "There's a great article on charity shops. The website's called 'Frugal Living'."

"I hear you're the expert at finding clothes in charity shops," Yolanda said to Pete, "Robin said you could give me some tips."

"One of my favourite subjects, I could keep going all night about that. Stop me if you get fed up."

Yolanda smiled, and he carried on.

"The most important thing is location. Only go to good areas where people have money. The best place near here is Whitstable. Full of DFLs."

"What does that mean?"

"Down From Londons – Londoners with holiday homes down

here," said Robin, "the property in Whitstable's pricey – more expensive than round here."

Pete spoke until the performance started. Yolanda watched him. Enthusiasm animated his sensitive features and his eyes sparkled. She was getting used to his idiosyncratic outfits. They suited him. He wore them unselfconsciously, not for effect, as she'd originally thought.

Most people she mixed with had no individual style. They conscientiously wore whichever designs and brands were in fashion, without originality. The aim was always to be 'on trend'. But she was no different. She had hardly selected an item of clothing for herself for decades, everything'd been chosen and supplied by Jackie and George.

As a lawyer, Yolanda had little scope for expression in her work clothes, but outside the office she could wear what she pleased. The idea appealed, but how to develop her own style? She ran her fingers through her hair with its incipient waves. This was a start. And so was the sweater and scarf. Even these small choices were liberating, showing what was possible.

The folk duo had pleasant voices, and sang well-known songs. The pub was packed and the audience enthusiastic. Yolanda sat back in her chair, letting the music wash over her. She didn't have to keep up with anyone, no one was judging her, except Melody. However, the logical side of her brain decided Melody wasn't important, and she dismissed her. Yolanda was used to being on guard, ready to protect herself from people who were in a position to affect her. But now she allowed herself to relax. The traditional folk songs struck a chord and she even found tears in her eyes.

In between songs, she asked Robin about the Folk Week.

"Folk Week's a kind of festival, it's a big thing down here. It's held every year in Broadstairs. It's amazing – lots of concerts and gigs and Morris dancing in the streets. There's a great craft market. People come from all over the country – there's camping."

“It's a great atmosphere,” said Tash, “and most things are free, apart from the big concerts. The gigs are mostly in pubs.”

“When is it?

“August.”

◆ ◆ ◆

Soon after nine the next morning, Yolanda’s phone rang. It was Molly, asking if she could come round to the flat to bring the bedding and towels and clean the place. Yolanda said she could come in an hour, and in half that time, was walking along the beach. The unbroken run of sunshine continued. It must be some kind of record, or maybe the weather down there was always better than London. A well-kept secret. A light wind blew back her hair, the pungent, cleansing breeze, flushing out the city grime from her lungs.

How wonderful to be able to walk on the beach every day. If she lived here, she wouldn't need to pay for a gym. When she started at the firm, reduced fees at a nearby gym were part of her employment package, but she found working out tedious and the surroundings uninspiring, and rarely used it. Jackie was right in her summing up of gyms, as ‘A good way to part fools from their money’. But walking by the sea was restorative and soothing. If she lived here, she could get a bike. Yolanda pictured herself riding on the promenade. In this vision, someone was riding alongside. Her companion came into focus, and she saw it was Pete. She wondered if he had a bike.

She couldn’t help comparing Pete with Mark. Pete wouldn't last five minutes in a London law firm. He didn’t have the killer instinct that Jackie admired so much. He was too nice. Was Mark too nice?

They’d met at the gym, when Yolanda literally threw herself at his feet. She was a sporadic exerciser, only visiting the gym when the prodding of her conscience couldn't be ignored. As she climbed on the treadmill, Yolanda was aware of a tall man jogging on the next machine. She took in dark wavy hair, a toned physique and a flash of blue eyes. Her pulse raced. Distracted by his good looks, she lost her footing and fell off the machine. She lay sprawled on the floor and Mark immediately came to her aid. Shaken but not hurt, she allowed him to take charge. He found a chair and offered to call a first aider. Yolanda shook her head. With one hand on the back of her the chair, Mark fended off offers of help from other exercisers.

When Yolanda came out of the changing room, Mark was waiting in the lobby and insisted on taking her home. That was how it started. The next day they met for lunch and Mark asked how she was feeling, with a concerned look in his black-fringed blue eyes. His interest in her welfare continued. Mark introduced her to a health drink that looked and tasted like liquidised grass, but he assured her it was much healthier than her usual sweetened latte. He promised she'd soon get used to it, and when she didn't, Yolanda drank the green sludge anyway, not wanting to hurt his feelings.

Mark was also a lawyer, a few years her senior. He worked at a larger firm than Nelson Riggs, and was already a team leader.

For such a handsome man, Mark carried his good looks lightly. Indulging in no lengthy grooming sessions, apart from a dash of citrus scented aftershave.

Yolanda had never been with someone who took such good care of her. Regularly frequenting the gym himself, Mark devised an exercise routine for her and encouraged her to carry it out regularly. She still found the activity tedious, but had to admit it was working. She lost weight, felt fitter and slept better.

Mark's flat was larger than hers, and nearer both of their offices. She found the immaculately decorated, spotlessly clean rooms sterile and intimidating, but somehow ended up spending most of her time there.

Mark's talents were boundless. He was a great cook, able to whip up healthy meals with ease. When she craved a fat and carb laden takeaway, Mark's frown and obvious disapproval deterred her. While he was away on business for a week, she gorged herself on pizza, curry and fried chicken, stuffing the forbidden foods into her mouth like a naughty child.

Soon after they met, Mark made it clear he didn't approve of the time and money Yolanda spent drinking in bars. The morning after a couple of heavy nights, he took her face in his hands and looked into her eyes. He shook his head sadly.

"Sweetheart, you need your beauty sleep, all this running around... you don't want to end up looking like..."

He mentioned a raddled celebrity. Yolanda recoiled. She'd never considered the harmful effects of her lifestyle. That was what she liked best about Mark. He was so caring. He sensed when she was tired or under the weather and was ready with a hug, a hot drink and a suggestion.

As she and Mark spent more time together, for Yolanda it was no hardship to relinquish nights out with so-called friends. Once a week, Mark would get together with his 'pals' – a group of friends from school or university. Yolanda couldn't stand them. They despised anyone who was different from them and weren't shy of expressing their prejudices. She knew Mark genuinely didn't share these views, but he never challenged them or defended his own principles.

"What do you see in them?" she asked.

Mark looked at her in surprise.

"What's wrong with them? They're a great bunch."

"They're arrogant, intolerant, racist, misogynistic..."

"I agree they're not exactly PC, but they're all damn good sorts."

After these meetings, Mark would roll back late and drunk. He didn't seem to be concerned about his beauty sleep.

He regularly brought work home to finish, working past

midnight, but he insisted that Yolanda go to bed at a reasonable hour.

"At your level, they don't pay you enough to bring work home, sweetheart."

He was right, but truthfully she preferred to do some tasks away from the noisy office, and her mind could function more clearly later in the evening. But mostly, Mark's censure discouraged her. He took better care of her than she did herself. He'd make a wonderful husband, and father...

◆ ◆ ◆

Yolanda's mind jumped forward several months. Mark was still as attentive and caring as ever, and she was doing well in her job. Her intelligence, dedication and willingness to work hard paid off. Gareth, her team leader, expressed his approval, and told her he was keeping an eye on her progress. One day he asked her to draft an important report for him. She was to focus on certain key points and keep it as short as possible. Yolanda wrote the first draft at the office, but wanted to perfect it at home. Luckily, Mark was meeting a client for dinner and wouldn't be in till late. Before he returned, she'd revised the report and was satisfied with the result. She turned off her laptop.

"You shouldn't have waited up, sweetheart. You look tired. Have you been working?"

"Only a short report for Gareth."

Mark's brow furrowed.

"He's a slave driver. Go off to bed now. Must get your beauty sleep."

Yolanda was tired, but her mind raced and she couldn't fall asleep. After tossing and turning for a while, she realised she needed to add something to the report. The light was still on in the living room, and Mark sat at the table. He'd switched on her laptop and was typing on the keyboard.

"What're you doing?"

He looked up.

"Just finishing this off. Won't be a minute," he returned to the screen.

Yolanda looked over his shoulder. Her report document was open and he was altering it.

"Why're you on my computer?" She spoke sharply, shock in her tone.

He stopped.

"I'm just tidying this up for you," he grinned, "Gareth is going to be impressed." He leaned back in the chair and stretched; his arms crossed behind his head. "You made a good start. I'm just adding the finishing touches."

Yolanda couldn't speak. She fought down the rising wave of rage, breathing fast with the effort.

"How did you get into the report? I know I switched off my laptop. How did you find out my password?"

He was still oblivious to her reaction.

"I always watch people entering their passwords. It's a useful habit."

"But Mark, this is confidential – you're a lawyer – you know you shouldn't... it's not professional!"

Mark clearly believed he'd done nothing wrong. He stretched again, rolled his shoulders to loosen the muscles and yawned.

"Don't worry, I won't say anything to anyone. Time for bed now. Or do you want to look at the improvements I've made, as you're up anyway?"

Yolanda was still silent, and finally Mark realised there was something wrong.

"Sweetheart, yours was good. I've just made it better."

Yolanda spoke in a choking voice, her face burning.

"But it won't be my work. I didn't ask for help."

"I can't understand why you're so upset. I'm more experienced than you. I thought I was helping. If you don't want me to, I won't do it again. Calm down, sweetheart. You're overreacting."

In the end Mark went off to bed, and Yolanda sat down at the table. Mark didn't know Gareth's instructions, so the focus of the report was wrong and it was too long. With trembling fingers, she began to type. When the piece was finished, Yolanda lay down on the sofa and slept fitfully, angry thoughts filling her dreams.

The next morning, Mark carried on as if nothing had happened. He didn't apologise and tried to kiss her goodbye. Yolanda turned her head away. He shrugged and went off to work. Her thoughts were in turmoil. She couldn't concentrate all morning, and dashed out at lunchtime to get a coffee. No liquid grass today. Only a sweet vanilla latte with whipped cream would do.

◆ ◆ ◆

That evening marked a turning point. The attractions of Mark's handsome face and muscular physique no longer concealed unpalatable aspects of his character and behaviour. His habit of taking her face in his hands to pronounce on her health, appearance and needs, with the epithet, 'sweetheart', now sounded patronising. For the first time she rebelled against their relentlessly healthy, but not always appetising diet, and brought back a pizza. Mark frowned, but said nothing. His disgruntled glances at the offending object banished Yolanda's appetite as quickly as one of Jackie's remarks, and most of the pizza ended up in the bin.

Yolanda dragged herself to the gym, and performed her exercise routine in a perfunctory manner. Mark noticed, but instead of bringing up the subject, he looked sorrowfully at her and stroked her hair. She disliked confrontations, but she almost hoped Mark would challenge her about the matter. At this stage, everything he did or said irritated her. She must get away, but couldn't face a discussion about her reasons, so she sent him a message.

Going back to my flat. Badly needs a thorough clean and tidy.

She knew he'd approve of the explanation.

Yolanda flopped onto her sofa with relief. She threw all her clothes on the floor and put on an old pair of pyjamas. Mark said nightwear was only for sleeping in, just the sort of thing Jackie would say. She sat up straight. She was letting Mark control her life in the same way as her mum. Why hadn't she seen it before?

From this new viewpoint, Mark's care and concern looked a lot like control and interference. As for his re-writing her report for Gareth, that was inexcusable, as well as unprofessional and possibly criminal. Worst of all, he didn't see he'd done anything wrong. Both Mark and Jackie treated Yolanda, a grown woman, like a helpless, naive child, to be patronised, protected and bullied. Her mum was one thing, but she didn't have to put up with such treatment from Mark. And she wouldn't.

She stayed at her flat for three days without communicating with Mark, ignoring his messages and calls. She knew the situation couldn't last, and on the third evening as she ate fried chicken and chips with her fingers, the doorbell rang. Mark stood there, his face full of concern.

"Sweetheart, what's going on?"

He raised his hands to take her face, but she recoiled. His hands fell to his sides.

"Hello Mark, come in."

He looked round the room. She evidently hadn't been house cleaning.

"Are you alright, sweetheart? I've been worried... you didn't answer the phone, reply to my messages..."

Now he was in front of her, Yolanda knew for sure her feelings for Mark had evaporated. She was icy cool. As if dealing with an awkward client, she rapidly assessed the situation, and chose her words deliberately.

"I've stayed away and haven't been in touch, because I needed space and time to think things over. Our relationship. Let's sit down."

"I don't understand. I thought we were happy... everything was going well... If you were unhappy, why didn't you tell me?"

"I didn't realise myself. But I do now."

"All I want is to take care of you."

"I know you mean well, and want to protect me, but I need to take care of myself."

Mark eyed the remains of her meal in its greasy container.

"You're not eating properly – that stuff's poison."

Yolanda showed no hint of the annoyance she felt.

"The odd unhealthy meal won't harm me."

Several unhealthy meals actually, but he didn't need to know that.

"Are you exercising? You've put on weight – and you were doing so well."

"Once again, my lifestyle's my choice."

Mark turned pale. His shoulders sagged.

"I don't understand," he muttered as if to himself.

Recognising his genuine sadness, Yolanda felt uncomfortable. She'd built him up in her mind as a bully, motivated by a desire to control and dominate her. Perhaps some of this was true, but mostly he saw her, a woman, as requiring a man's protection and wanted to provide it.

"Mark," she said more gently, "I know you're a good person. But we have different outlooks on life. Although it's painful now, it would be worse if we found out later."

He blinked as if trying to understand, and stood up slowly, staggering a little.

"If that's how you feel, there's nothing more to be said."

His face was white.

"I don't understand," he burst out, "I always try to be the good guy, do the right thing, treat women properly... I don't know how else to be. But it seems that's not what they want..."

He stood up straight and held out his hand.

"I'm sorry how things have worked out Yolanda. I wish you well."

She shook his hand. She had no regrets, but couldn't help feeling respect for his dignity.

◆ ◆ ◆

Yolanda sighed. But that was all in the past. As she walked on the firm, damp sand, the sound of the waves softly swooshing in the background, she looked to the future and imagined a new a life in these idyllic surroundings. She knew the weather wouldn't always be good. A sea view also meant high winds, and the coastline would be bleak in the winter. No bike riding then. What could her life look like away from London? Of course, Jackie would think she was mad even to consider it. Having worked so hard to gain her current position, any move that didn't involve climbing the ladder would be unthinkable. Yolanda remembered Robin asking what being successful meant to her. Detached from the emotion of her mum's phone call, Yolanda realised she'd never considered the question before. She knew what Jackie's idea was, but what was her own?

She had to earn a living, but how did she feel about her job? With surprise, she decided she liked the work, the intellectual challenge, attention to detail and sense of achievement. She enjoyed practising law. She even liked some of her colleagues and clients. It was the nature of the firm she disliked. The atmosphere of unbridled rivalry, backstabbing and distrust. An element of competition was acceptable, but there was little genuine teamwork, or consideration for others. Despite uneasy truces, co-workers were regarded as competitors in a race where the weaker fell by the wayside and no-one gave them a second thought. She imagined a company without that pressure. Where high standards of work were required and staff were dedicated, but everyone worked together and supported each other. Was this a utopian dream, or could it exist within a law firm? Probably not in a high-level London firm, but maybe a local company, where one had the chance to give to the community – taking on Legal Aid cases, for example. Naturally, salaries in such an organisation would be lower, but as long as they were high enough.

Where to live? Seeing the cost of property in Westgate, Yolanda knew she could make money if she sold her London flat and bought in this area. Her logical brain took charge. That was too big a commitment. However, there was nothing to stop her renting out her London flat and exchanging it for a small place down here. The difference in rents would provide a source of income. She was already recognising ways she could reduce her expenses. This would be an essential part of the process. She'd have to crunch the numbers.

Yolanda had walked all the way along the promenade to the outskirts of Margate. Drinking coffee at a beach front cafe, she continued her reverie. The attractions of this area were obvious and numerous, but what were the downsides? What would she miss if she left London? Being as honest and objective as she could, Yolanda was surprised that her first thought was her art class and her friend Claudia. There must be art classes down here, Robin or Penny Paynter would know. And Claudia could come and visit – Joseph would love the beach.

London had an incredible richness of art, but she could go back to visit for the day. The city was readily accessible by car or train. Yolanda forced herself to come down to earth. She'd spent so little time here, there might be many relevant factors of which she was unaware. It would be crazy to change her whole life on the basis of a short stay. Or would it, asked a small voice in her head?

◆ ◆ ◆

When she returned to the flat, Yolanda arranged a few flowers from the vase on the dining table in a mug. She took the flowers and her art materials – in their new tote bag – out on the balcony and settled down to draw. She tried to recapture the state of flow she'd achieved, drawing intuitively, what she felt rather than saw. While her hand was drawing, Yolanda's mind returned to Beth Winthrop. Robin had asked what she was going to do next? What **could** she do next was a better question?

Since learning of Beth's disappearance, Yolanda was even more curious about the expression on her face in the newspaper photograph and Margery's portrait. What was Beth feeling? What emotion had the camera and the artist captured? Did this have any connection with her disappearance? More importantly, what had happened to Beth? Was she alive? There were also the questions Fearne had raised, why her parents only had that one, unnerving photograph and why Beth and Amber had gone away together if they weren't friends?

So many questions, but how and where could Yolanda find answers? If the police hadn't discovered a solution at the time, how could she, an ordinary person, hope to do so many years later? This was truly a cold case. She continued drawing while she thought, not aiming for a 'good' picture, just allowing her hand to move over the pages of the sketchbook.

She could speak to Beth's parents, if they still lived in the same place. The article gave their full names and she should be able to track them down. But what to say? How could she persuade them to talk to her?

CHAPTER 5

The next day Yolanda awoke to grey skies and rain slashing against her bedroom window. The weather had finally turned. She looked out of the window at the sea. What a difference. The benevolent blue presence had been replaced by a dark, angry force. The tame beast had turned wild, working itself up into a frenzy. Flashes of white appeared on the surface like glimpses of teeth. The incoming waves attacked the shore in unrelenting onslaughts.
No muesli on the balcony today. What should she do? With the change in the weather, her mood altered. The English seaside was fine in the sunshine, but on a day like this... And she was staying for another week. Yolanda almost hoped someone from the office would phone and demand her immediate return. There wasn't even any cleaning, Molly had done a good job.

After breakfast, Yolanda put on a load of washing and looked round the flat. In the small hallway, she spotted something on the floor. It was the latest copy of the *East Kent Gazette*; someone must've delivered it. She turned over the pages. Would there be an interesting photograph? The best one was of a local MP who'd just died. The man had a face that would have attracted Margery's attention. Furrowed with deep lines and a thoughtful expression.

She opened her box of pencils. She coloured in the photograph, exaggerating the man's features as Margery had done. She examined the effect and an idea began to take shape in her mind. Using luminous stained-glass colours, she could draw stylised portraits. Not of the biblical figures and saints usually represented in church windows, but current figures – celebrities or others in the news. A series of these would make an effective, eye-catching display for the art show.

Her phone rang and she realised it was twelve o'clock.

"Hi Yolanda, it's Fearne O'Keefe here. I've got some information for you."

"Hi, that's quick work."

"I don't let the grass grow under my feet. First of all, the musician who was the police suspect was called Jango James – that was his stage name. His real name's James Perrot and I have his phone number. He lives in Croydon and works in insurance. I'm sending all this in an email.

"The friend, Amber, is married and she's now Amber Mitchell. She still lives in Chelmsford and works in a building society. Beth's parents still live in the same house."

"Thanks so much, I really appreciate it."

"I did some digging around and called in a couple of favours. I'm seriously thinking of doing a follow up article. There've been a number of unsolved disappearances over the years. So, if it helps, you can mention the *Gazette* and say you're working with me on that.

"Thanks so much. I'll get right onto it and let you know anything I find out."

At last, information to work on.

◆ ◆ ◆

Yolanda tackled James first. She rang his number, and introduced herself. She explained she was writing an article for the *Gazette* as Fearne suggested. There was silence at the other end of the phone. After a long pause, he spoke.

"I don't want anything to do with it." He sounded agitated. "I don't want to go over all that again. I can't..."

Yolanda was nonplussed. She couldn't force the man to talk to her, but thinking quickly, she went on.

"Mr Perrot," she said in her best legal tones, calm, but firm, "I'm just checking the facts. I have the original article to work from, but I'm sure you wouldn't want anything incorrect to go into the new article."

"Why're you raking all that up again. And I don't see why you need to mention me at all."

"I do understand, Mr Perrot, but you were involved in the original case. I have to be in your area tomorrow, could I speak to you briefly – just to make sure I have the facts straight?"

"Well, I don't know. I suppose... I can only spare a few minutes."

"That's fine, what time would suit you? Shall I come to your home?"

"No, no, absolutely not. You can come to the office. Two o'clock. But I won't have long."

◆ ◆ ◆

In the pub that night, Yolanda told Robin about her idea for the art exhibition. When the others heard, they joined in the discussion. Even Melody had something to say.

"Melody's a graphic designer in her spare time, she makes cards and cool invitations," said Robin.

"I'm not as boring as I look," said Melody, but she seemed pleased.

Tash mentioned that traditional stained-glass windows had to contain a certain proportion of white to balance the effect of the colours. Robin recommended a type of card for mounting, that Paynter's stocked. Unused to this kind of discussion, Yolanda was pleased to have her idea taken seriously.

Yolanda was glad she'd brought one business outfit with her, following her mum's adage, 'Always be prepared for a meeting', as she set off for Croydon the next day.

She arrived at James Perrot's office just before two, and as she switched her phone onto silent, she noticed Fearne had sent an email with an attachment. She didn't want to keep James waiting. She'd check the email later, hopefully it didn't contain anything important.

James Perrot wore dark-framed glasses, an innocuous tie and looked the epitome of a respectable insurance broker. She saw photos of his wife and children on the desk, when he ushered her quickly into his office.

"I'm not at all comfortable about this," he said, "is it really necessary?"

Yolanda ignored his question, put on her most efficient manner and took out a notebook.

"This won't take long, Mr Perrot, let's get started shall we. I understand you performed as Jango James – you were a singer?"

"Yes, and I played the guitar."

"Do you remember the first time you saw Beth?"

"They said she was there at my first gig, in a pub, but I didn't remember seeing her. The first session's always fraught, getting set up, the equipment, a new audience. She may've been there, I don't know."

"That's fine. Do you remember seeing her any other times?"

"Yes, I told them all this. It's upsetting to bring it up again." He sighed. "Yes, she came to the next gig I did. In one of the other pubs. I only remember because she asked for a request. I didn't get so many of those, not early in the week."

"What was the song she asked for?"

"That was the other thing – it wasn't one of the usual ones. It wasn't that well known and not especially popular. It was called 'Now Is the Time."

"Did she say why she wanted it?"

"No, I don't think so. But what's all this got to do with..."

"Just trying to get the facts clear, Mr Perrot. Do you remember, was she alone?"

"I'm not sure, I don't remember. There might've been another girl."

"Did you see Beth again?"

"I think she came to a gig in another pub the next night. It was so long ago. And she came to a session I did in a cafe in the morning. There weren't so many people, so I remembered her – it was the hair. She was by herself. She asked me for a request again. The same song."

"Could she have asked for the request as an excuse to talk to you?"

"They went through all this at the time. Absolutely not. Sometimes girls do... you can always tell. But in this case, it was only the song. She wasn't interested in anything else."

"What about you, were you interested in her?"

"No, she wasn't my type. I found her a bit weird. That hair, almost hiding her face. Like she was looking out from a curtain. Besides, I'd learned not to get to close to fans."

"Was that the last time you saw her?"

"No, it was the evening. I don't know whether it was that night or the next. I was getting used to her by then. There were often some loyal fans after a few gigs. They came to everything I did. So, I wasn't surprised when she asked for the request again. I think I played it next, it was the next song. Usually you can't, you play the request later. But this time I played it straight away. She just stood there, not moving. She was quite close and I could see her expression, looking through that hair. She had this look in her eyes – I can't describe it."

"Was she upset, surprised..."

"No, nothing like that. It was almost – religious. I know that sounds crazy – it was just a folk song and not a very good one. She stood there like that while I was playing. Then at the end, she just walked straight out of the pub. Usually if someone's requested a song they applaud, stay around. She just went straight out."

"Could she have seen someone? Over your shoulder or in the pub?"

"Maybe, I don't know. I never saw her again. And the police hounded me and..."

He put his hands over his face.

"It was terrible. They seemed to think I'd... They kept on and on. They tore my van to pieces. I was sleeping in a caravan. It was the worst time of my life." He shuddered.

"What happened afterwards?"

"They had to let me go. There was no evidence. They said she'd run off with someone to France."

"What do you think really happened to Beth?"

"I don't know, I don't know! The whole business affected me very badly. I never sang or played another note. My wife doesn't know anything about it. I can't tell you any more."

The man was shaking.

"Thank you very much for your help, Mr Perrot. I'm sorry to upset you."

"Just go," he said.

Yolanda switched the sound back on her phone and checked the email from Fearne.

How're you getting on? I've done some more digging; thought

you might be interested in this. It might help if you get to talk to James Perrot.

There was a newspaper article attached, dated three years before Beth's disappearance, from the Cambridge News.

Missing girl found safe and sound.

Linsey March, 18, reported missing at the Cambridge Folk Festival, has turned up safe and well. Linsey said she'd been staying with her boyfriend in his caravan. She had met Jango James, a performer at the festival, for the first time at the opening concert. Mr James, 28, was not available for comment.

Yolanda stared at the article. So, James had a connection with another girl who went missing at a Folk Festival. If only she'd checked Fearne's email before speaking to him, she could've asked questions and observed his reaction to this other case. Even though Linsey had turned up unharmed, when James was a suspect in the Winthrop case, the police would've taken a special interest – questioned him more extensively. That would explain his distress. But did it mean anything else?

◆ ◆ ◆

When Yolanda got to the pub that night, Robin hadn't arrived. Pete smiled at her and pointed at the chair beside him. Andy leaned over trying to attract her attention.

"He wants to show you his wip," said Tash.

"Hey, Tash," said Andy in protest.

Yolanda looked puzzled. Was that a euphemism?

"Wip, work in progress," said Pete with a grin, "the great graphic novel."

Robin arrived, out of breath.

"Sorry I'm late, but –" she was smiling, "I had a phone call. Good news."

The others looked at her expectantly.

“I've got an exhibition, it's during Folk Week.”

“Great news, well done,” said Tash, “where?”

“Oh, just a local pub.” Robin’s expression indicated suppressed excitement.

“Which pub?” asked Andy.

“Oh, only The Sportsman.” said Robin.

The responses were immediate and excited.

“Wow, Robin, The Sportsman!” said Melody.

Pete turned to Yolanda.

“The Sportsman's this great gastro pub, it's famous. In Seasalter near Whitstable. People come from all over – you have to book weeks in advance. Everyone wants an exhibition there; it's a great showcase and people buy.”

“Yes,” said Robin, “seriously pricey, you need a mortgage to eat there.”

“I'm sure Yolanda could afford to eat there,” said Melody.

The others stared at her.

“What do you mean?” said Robin.

“Just what I said. She's got plenty of money. The Sportsman's just her sort of place. She's not skint like you. Have you asked her about her job?”

“Yes,” said Robin, “she works in an office. Anyway, what does that matter?”

“You're so naive, Robin, you've only known her a few days. Her coat must’ve cost an arm and a leg.”

There was an uncomfortable silence. Yolanda stiffened and Pete put his hand on her arm. Her legal training kicked in and she thought quickly. She looked at Melody dispassionately, and spoke calmly without annoyance or anger. Pete removed his hand.

"Melody's quite right." She paused after saying this, and deliberately moved her gaze around the group. "I'm a lawyer. I work for a law firm in London." Her matter-of-fact tone diffused the effect of Melody's outburst. "In my spare time I'm an artist. Just like you, Melody." She paused again. "I came down here for a break, and to get inspiration for my art. It's been marvellous. I was lucky enough to meet Robin and now all of you. I've never met a group of people who're so welcoming, friendly and non-judgmental."

Yolanda's words and tone deflated Melody. She looked down and said nothing.

"Let's drink a toast," Yolanda said, "to Robin for her exhibition and a thank you to everyone.

"That was nice of you," Pete said to Yolanda, when the general conversation had started up again. She could still feel the pressure of his fingers on her arm.

"I meant it. These few days down here have made me think about things. My life. How I've been living. There's something about it down here. The people are different. Their values. They're friendly and helpful. I've never experienced such kindness before – from people who hardly know me."

"That's true," Pete said, "we all felt it. None of us are from this area, we all came here and we stayed." He stared into the distance. "When I came, I wasn't in great shape. I was lucky, I met someone. She helped me get back on track. Her name was Madi and she was like a mother to me. Sometimes your real family can let you down. Strangers can be kinder."

Yolanda was curious, but didn't want to pry.

She thought about Tony. Since she could remember, she missed having a dad. She envied the other families she saw around her. George, Jackie's friend who owned the dress shop, was also a successful businesswoman, but she'd been married to Tony since she was twenty, although they had no children. Tony was the opposite to George and Jackie. Laid-back and unambitious, he took life as it came. He worked as a carpenter, never expanding his business as George and Jackie urged.

Yolanda loved Tony, she liked to pretend he was her dad. The pair were good friends and he was the one person in whom she could confide. Because George was so similar to Jackie, he understood Yolanda's situation.

"George is the one with all the brains in this family," he would say to her with a wink.

At Yolanda's graduation from university, Jackie took a rare day off and came with George. Yolanda said she wanted Tony there as well, but was told he wasn't available. She was surprised and disappointed. When she was working in London, she never heard from him and she thought she'd mistaken his attention for genuine liking. He'd merely been kind to a kid.

◆ ◆ ◆

When she got home, her phone rang. It was Robin.

"Hi, sorry to ring so late, but I wanted to explain about Melody. You must've wondered why I didn't say anything when she spoke to you like that. She was out of order."

"It's fine, I'm not –"

"You've every right to be annoyed. She shouldn't have said those things. But Melody has some problems. I'm telling you this in confidence, right?"

"Of course."

"Before she came down here – it must be five or six years ago, she had some kind of breakdown. She was quite sick. That was the reason she came here, to get away from things, pressure. She's been much better, but she's still fragile. Up and down. At the moment she's down, so we try and make allowances for her.

When she's up she's a lovely person."

"Thanks for telling me, Robin. I understand. Really, it's fine. I'm sorry I didn't tell you I was a lawyer, but it didn't seem relevant. I hope you don't think that –"

"No, I don't care about people's jobs. Unless it's something arty, creative, I'm not interested."

How kind Robin was. What a good friend to Melody. Yolanda thought about her mum's attitude to illness. In spite of Jackie's unhealthy lifestyle, she hadn't known a day's illness in her life, and had no sympathy for other sufferers, believing they were just weak. Yolanda remembered being sent home from school on more than one occasion with a note from the teacher saying she was sick and shouldn't be sent to school until she'd recovered.

◆ ◆ ◆

The next day, Yolanda was on the road again, this time to Chelmsford, to see Amber and hopefully Beth's parents. On the phone, Amber had reacted differently to James Perrot. She was quite willing to talk to Yolanda and agreed to meet for lunch – for which Yolanda gave the impression the *Gazette* would pay.

Amber arrived at the expensive restaurant in good time, clearly impressed by her surroundings. She had over-processed blonde hair and wore a navy 'chain store' suit with a pink blouse. Yolanda was pleased when Amber accepted a gin and tonic, hoping the alcohol would help the conversation.

"So, did you say you're writing an article about Beth?"

"Yes, it's a follow up, looking at how she disappeared. You're an important witness."

"So, will the newspaper pay any money for my story?"

Yolanda was ready for this.

"*The Gazette*'s budget is limited – you know how it is these days – I'll bring the subject up with Ms O'Keeffe, but I can't promise anything."

This vague statement satisfied Amber.

"I've studied the facts in the original investigation, and there're some things I'd like to get clear. You and Beth went to the Folk Week together, whose idea was it to go?"

"It was mine. You see, I'd been the year before. With another girl. Camping."

"What made you decide to go again?"

Amber smiled faintly, and turned pink.

"I met a guy – me and my friend – we met these two guys. They were really nice. We met them at the beginning and we spent the whole week together. We kept in touch afterwards. They lived up north, Liverpool. Scott, he came to see me and I went to see him. We met up at other places." Amber had a faraway look in her eyes.

"Then we kind of drifted apart. Long distance romance, you know. I tried to call him a few times, but there was a problem with his phone. I couldn't get through."

"You wanted to go to the Folk Week again, you thought...?"

"I thought maybe Scott would come again. I might bump into him there. But my friend, the one I went with, she wanted to go to Spain with our other friends. They wanted me to go as well, but I thought I'd have another go at Broadstairs. I couldn't find anyone else to go with. I wouldn't go by myself, I'm not that sort of girl. I couldn't walk into a pub by myself or a cafe, or sit on the beach." Amber's high-pitched voice was grating.

"How did you come to go with Beth? Were you two good friends?"

"No – I hardly knew her. But I was getting desperate, and she came to work in the shop where I worked. We were in an art class together at school. But I didn't know her. I mentioned that I was thinking of going to the Folk Week. She'd nowhere else to go, had no money but was fed up staying at home all summer. It was a cheap holiday, camping and most of the gigs were free. I had the tent and a car. It seemed a good idea at the time."

"How did it turn out?"

Amber frowned.

"We went to a gig the first night. Beth seemed alright – a bit quiet. Two guys started talking to us and she suddenly ran out, without saying anything. It was rude.

"The next night we went to another gig. That's when we saw that guy – the one the police thought... He was a singer and played the guitar. His name was Jango something. I kept my eyes open for Scott, but he wasn't there."

"Did you talk about this guy Jango at all? Did Beth say anything about him?"

"No. She wasn't much of a talker. That was part of the problem. I like a good chat, and a laugh. Guys don't come up to you if you're just sitting there. It doesn't make a good impression."

"What happened after that?"

"We had different ideas about what we wanted to do, Beth and me. The year before, we went on the beach in the mornings – it was great, loads of people would show up. I had this bikini." She smiled at the memory. "It was all about getting a suntan, having a laugh."

"What about Beth, did she like sunbathing?"

"No. She wouldn't sit in the sun. It might've been something to do with her skin – she was very fair. And she always wore a tee shirt and jeans on the beach. And it wasn't a fitted tee shirt – it was, like, two sizes too big." Amber looked down at her own tight pink top. "She didn't have a bikini or even a costume. Basically, Beth had no idea how to dress, how to make the most of herself. She had all that hair, but there was too much. It just hung down. If it was me, I'd have had it straightened – guys don't like curly hair. Some of the girls in the shop wanted to give her a makeover, but she wasn't interested.

"So, on the beach, she sat by herself in the shade and read a book or did drawings. She never spoke to anyone."

"What did you think about that?"

"It wasn't much fun for me, I can tell you. I didn't like sitting by myself. And then in the evenings, I like to go to different gigs, different performers. And I wanted to keep an eye out in case Scott... Well Beth only wanted to go to gigs where that Jango was playing. I went along with her the next night, she sat there again with nothing to say, her face almost covered up by that hair. I got really fed up. And then when Jango came on, she perked up. After a few numbers, she went up and asked him to play a song. I could see what she was up to."

"What was that?"

"She liked him, of course. She thought that if she asked him for a request, he would start talking to her. But anyone could see he wasn't interested."

"Are you sure about that? Sure he wasn't interested?"

"Yes, it was obvious. He didn't give her a second look."

"Is it possible Beth was only interested in the song?"

"Of course not. Who would be that interested in a song? Jango wasn't such a great singer, and his songs were nothing special. No, she was after him all right. But she should've realised he didn't want to know, and moved on."

"What happened next?"

"The next day, Beth said she wanted to go to a gig in the morning, there was something on in a cafe. It was that guy again, Jango. I wanted to go to the beach. We had a row, she didn't understand why we couldn't each do our own thing, why did we have to be together all the time. But I didn't want to go around by myself, that's why I asked her to come."

"What happened next?"

"I can't remember; I think I went off to the beach and I don't know what she did. I don't think I saw her during the day. In the evening she was in the tent. I asked her what she was doing and she said she was going to another pub where Jango was playing. I got annoyed and I told her straightaway she was wasting her time, he wasn't interested."

"What did she say?"

"Nothing. She didn't answer. Then she just walked out. It was really rude. I was telling her for her own good. She didn't seem to know anything about guys."

"Did you see her again after that?"

"No, I went off to another pub. I met up with some of the girls from the beach, they were a real laugh, good fun. And a few guys came over. I think we went on somewhere else. I can't really remember. I got back pretty late, but Beth wasn't there. She hadn't come back by the morning. I just thought she'd hooked up with someone. So, I didn't see her again. She left her sleeping bag and towel and other stuff in the tent. I thought she'd come back and get them. To be honest, I thought she was really rude. I'd asked her to come, it was my car, my tent, I thought she should've told me she was going. I was pretty fed up with her."

"You weren't worried when she didn't turn up again, then?"

"No, I was sure she'd gone off with someone."

"Did you try and phone her?"

"Of course. I kept ringing her, but her phone was turned off. I guessed she was with some guy – busy – you know and didn't want to talk to me.

"What happened then?"

"I had a better time for the rest of the week. I went around with the girls and guys I told you about. Scott never turned up and nothing else serious, just a bit of fun. But a few months later I met Danny – my husband."

"I understand that Beth's parents reported her missing, when she didn't return home after the end of the week."

"Yes, her mum called me. Asked me where she was. I didn't like to tell on her. I thought she'd be home soon and her mum and dad didn't need to know anything. Her mum got annoyed, saying why didn't I tell them. But Beth was an adult, she wasn't my responsibility. And then the police made me come back to Broadstairs. It was really annoying, my boss wasn't happy, me having to take time off just after I'd been on holiday."

"What did the police ask you?"

"The same sort of things you've been asking. They seemed to think that Jango guy had done away with Beth. I don't know why they thought she was dead. They never found her body. It was much more likely she went off with someone. There were all sorts of guys hanging around at the gigs – if you weren't too fussy."

At that point, the waiter came over and cleared away their plates.

"Would you like coffee, ladies, and can I tempt you to a liqueur?"

Yolanda caught a flash of interest in Amber's eyes.

"What do you say, Amber, what do you fancy?"

"I don't usually indulge – but if the paper's paying – I'll have a Baileys, thanks."

Amber sat back and savoured the creamy drink. Her face was flushed and her eyes lost focus.

Yolanda looked at her.

"What did you really think of Beth?"

If she'd hoped to catch Amber off guard, she succeeded.

"If you want the truth, she was a stuck-up bitch. Thought she was better than me. I saw the way she looked down her nose when I..."

Amber recollected herself. What she was saying and to whom. But Yolanda had seen enough. A look in Amber's eyes of spite, even hatred, towards Beth. The look was brief but unmistakeable. The shrill outburst showed her true feelings.

Amber checked her phone. "I'd better go now, or I'll be late back. Is that all you wanted to know?"

Her face was red and she staggered a little as she walked out.

Now Yolanda had a clear picture of the relationship between Amber and Beth. They hardly knew each other and had gone to Broadstairs together for convenience, even, as Amber said, desperation. Probably on both sides. She expected Beth to fit in with her plans and act in the same way her friend had done the previous year. Amber made it clear her main interest in Folk Week was to gain the attention of men. For that she needed a partner, someone who would fit in, play along. When she realised Beth had other ideas, Amber ended up hating her companion.

It wasn't clear what Beth expected from the holiday. What was Beth really like? What were her interests? Who were her real friends? What were her hopes and dreams? And most of all, why did she have that gut wrenching expression in the photograph?

CHAPTER 6

The only way to find out the answers to these questions was to talk to Beth's parents. Tired and overwhelmed by Amber's revelations, her head aching from the whiny voice, Yolanda had little enthusiasm for this meeting, but it wasn't worth coming back another day. Part of her hoped no one was home. When the doorbell wasn't answered immediately, she turned to go with relief, but then the door opened.
A woman in her early sixties stood in the doorway. She had faded auburn hair.

"Can I help you?"

"Mrs Winthrop? My name is Yolanda Blake... I'm from the *East Kent Gazette*. I'm writing an article on... a follow up article to..."

Mrs Winthrop stared at her.

"East Kent, isn't that where...? Are you talking about Beth?"

"Yes Mrs Winthrop, I'm sorry to trouble you, I know this must be painful. I'm writing an article about your daughter's disappearance, and I want to make sure I have the facts straight. We don't want anything to go in the article that's incorrect."

"I suppose you'd better come in."

Wishing she was miles away, Yolanda entered the house. They sat in a living room which was tastefully furnished in shades of grey, with a modern sofa and large TV. A collection of photographs covered the coffee table. Mrs Winthrop saw Yolanda looking at them.

“My daughter Karen and her family and my son Brett. She's got two children and he's got three. They're all doing very well.” Linda Winthrop’s pleasant contralto was a welcome contrast to Amber’s shrill tones.

“Mrs Winthrop, I hope it's not too difficult, do you mind if I ask a few questions? Just to get my facts straight,” she repeated.

“What do you want to know?”

“What sort of girl was Beth?”

The answer came quickly.

“Difficult.” Mrs Winthrop gazed at the photographs. “You see we had Karen and Brett, a boy and a girl. They were as good as gold. No trouble. Happy children. Then Beth came along. Even as a little girl she was different. Karen was such a sunny child, always smiling and Brett was the same. Played together nicely, they did. I didn't know what to do with Beth. I used to call her the changeling, like she was someone else's child, given to us by mistake. She got upset easily – over nothing. Brett, he used to tease her – all brothers tease little sisters. I told her to take no notice. Karen gave as good as she got, but Beth... He didn't mean it.

“As Beth got older, it was worse. Karen had a nice group of girlfriends, they’d come round all the time, laughing and joking. But she worked hard at school – did her homework first. And Brett – he was always top of the class. Every prize giving, we were so proud. He went on to university in London, he's an optometrist.” She pronounced the word carefully, “an optician. He has his own shop, it’s in the best part of Chelmsford. And Karen did well at school too, she went to university in Birmingham. She’s a teacher. She teaches history. It's a good job – with the kids – the holidays.”

Mrs Winthrop’s eyes kept returning to the photos on the table.

"And what about Beth?"

Mrs Winthrop frowned.

"You'd think with such good examples, she'd do well at school. But she didn't bother. Didn't work. The teachers said she was bright enough, but she didn't pay attention in class. Half the time she didn't do her homework. It used to make Phil, my husband, mad. She was capable, but she didn't put any effort in, didn't try. He couldn't stand it."

"Was she happy at school?"

"I don't know. You never knew with Beth; she wouldn't talk about things. Just hid behind her hair."

"Did she have any hobbies, interests, anything she was good at?"

"She liked art. The art teacher said she was good, but that never led anywhere. She wouldn't put the work in. There was swimming. She used to be a good little swimmer, they said she had potential. She had the right build – tall – she and Brett take after Phil. Karen takes after me.

"We thought that might work out, they said she could go far, if she had coaching. Phil took her three times a week to the pool. There was a coach, he worked with the top young swimmers in the county. It was hard for Phil driving her around after a day's work, but he was prepared to do it. To help her succeed at something.

"But like everything else, she didn't have the commitment. What did he call it? The staying power. After all his efforts, when she got to about eleven or twelve, she suddenly stopped. Wouldn't even get in the water. Wouldn't give a reason. Phil was livid."

Linda paused.

"It was about that time, when she reached – you know – puberty," she blushed. "I wanted to get her some nice clothes, a better hairstyle. But she got angry, all she wanted to wear was those big tee shirts. So ugly. I did think then, maybe there was something wrong with her. It wasn't normal. Karen at that age – well most girls – are interested in clothes. I wanted to take her to see someone, a doctor, specialist. But Phil wouldn't hear of it. He said she was just doing it – playing up – for attention and the best thing to do was ignore her. I still don't know if that was the right thing to do."

Yolanda looked at one photo among the collection. A tall, smiling man with his arm round a younger version of Linda, a girl, Karen and a tall teenage boy, Brett. Where was Beth? Was this a family trying to cope with a problem child, or was something else behind the happy façade?

"Did Beth have friends?"

Mrs Winthrop thought for a while. "When she was a teenager, she had a few friends. Weirdos, Brett called them that. There was this girl, she wore black lipstick and black clothes – a ring through her nose." Mrs Winthrop wrinkled her own nose in disgust. "And there was another one, peculiar, couldn't tell if he was a boy or a girl. Phil didn't like them coming to the house. He told Beth he didn't want a bunch of weirdos around the place. So, they stopped coming." she frowned.

"The school – they wanted Beth to speak to a... what do you call it? A counsellor. But Phil wasn't having that. He said it would make her worse, fill her head with a lot of nonsense. He said she'd grow out of it."

"What about after school, did Beth go to university?"

"Not her. She wasn't interested. And she didn't get the grades. Phil told her; she'd have to get a job. She could live at home, but she'd have to pay her way."

"Did she get a job?"

"She had a few jobs – none of them were good. Waitressing, working in a shop. Brett got her a job – he didn't have his own shop then – in an opticians, as a receptionist. We were pleased about that, thought it might lead somewhere. But something happened…"

Mrs Winthrop screwed up her eyes.

"What was it?" she murmured. "Beth wouldn't come out of her room – she stayed there for a couple of weeks. We didn't know what happened. Phil spoke to her, but she wouldn't say.

"It was when Karen was expecting her first. She was having a difficult time. Phil said Beth wanted the attention. Because Karen needed help – with the pregnancy – she felt left out."

"What happened then?"

"After a couple of weeks, she just came out of her room. To be honest, I was that busy with Karen, I didn't have time – Beth seemed alright."

"Did she have any boyfriends?"

Mrs Winthrop shook her head. "Not that I knew of. Now Karen, when she started going with Paul..." Mrs Winthrop's eyes went straight to the photos again.

"Then Beth went on holiday to Broadstairs, for the Folk Week. With Amber. Did you know her?"

"No, Beth had a job in the shop where Amber worked. She came back one day and said she was going on holiday with Amber. She knew her from school. Amber came round once. We were surprised, she looked quite normal. Phil said to Beth, 'It's nice to see you with a normal friend for once.' We thought it was a good sign. And off they went. Amber had a car."

"Did you hear from Beth while she was away?"

"I don't think so – she was only in Kent – there was no reason to talk on the phone. Though if it'd been Karen, she'd be ringing every day, letting me know what she was doing." She smiled.

"What happened next?"

"Beth was supposed to be back. We couldn't understand it. We thought maybe they'd got delayed, had a problem with the car. I tried to ring her, but I couldn't get through. I thought maybe her phone was broken, or she'd lost it. But when she wasn't back by the next day, I phoned Amber. She wasn't very helpful; said she hadn't seen Beth in days. In the end we reported it to the police. Didn't see what else to do. We had to go down there to the police station in Margate. They asked us all about Beth. Amber was there as well."

Yolanda looked at Mrs Winthrop, she couldn't understand the woman. She was talking about the disappearance of her twenty-three-year-old daughter. About the girl's possible death, her last few hours. She didn't seem distressed. She was far less upset than James Perrot. Yolanda was at a loss to understand.

"What did the police do?"

"They got hold of this chap – he was a musician – playing at the festival. They said Beth was talking to him. Was keen on him."

"Was she interested in music?"

Mrs Winthrop's brow wrinkled.

"I don't remember specially."

"It seems that she asked the musician to play a certain song," Yolanda said, "she asked several times for the same song."

Mrs Winthrop shook her head.

"I don't know anything about that."

"Forgive me, Mrs Winthrop, but what did you think had happened to Beth?"

Yolanda could've been asking Mrs Winthrop if she thought it was going to rain.

"No idea. It was a mystery to me. Phil said she must've gone off with someone. He was very angry, we had to spend a lot of time at the police station. He said it was a waste, the police should've found her. He said they were useless."

"What did you think?"

Again, that calm reply.

"I didn't know what to think."

Yolanda couldn't help herself.

"And you never found out what happened to Beth, that must've been devastating?"

Mrs Winthrop turned surprised eyes to Yolanda.

"Sorry? What did you say?"

"You never found out what happened to Beth."

"But I thought you knew." Mrs Winthrop stared at her. "We did find out what happened to her. We got a letter. Yes, it must've been a couple of months later. We got a letter from her."

"Forgive me, Mrs Winthrop, you received a letter from Beth two months after she disappeared?"

"Yes, that's what I said. A letter arrived – Folkestone postmark. She wrote that she was okay. She was sorry to cause any trouble. She was starting a new life and she wasn't coming home again. There were some nasty things, about how she'd always been unhappy, her only chance was to start again. She said we weren't to contact her, she never wanted to hear from us again."

Yolanda sat back processing this fresh information.

"Are you sure the letter was from Beth?"

"Yes, it was in her handwriting. I'd know it anywhere."

"Didn't you think it odd that she wrote a letter instead of phoning?"

Mrs Winthrop considered the question. She shrugged.

"I couldn't say."

Yolanda struggled to make sense of the situation.

"Mrs Winthrop, did you inform the police when you heard from Beth?"

"I can't remember. No, I don't think we did. We didn't think of it.

They hadn't been very good."

"Do you still have the letter?"

For the first time, Mrs Winthrop looked uneasy.

"No. Phil told me to tear it up. He was very angry. Wasting our time like that – then writing all those nasty things."

She looked down. Yolanda felt she was hiding something. There was no point in staying any longer, but she had one more question to ask.

"Do you have a photograph of Beth?"

Mrs Winthrop's eyes immediately went to the collection on the coffee table.

"I don't think so. She hated having her picture taken – from when she was quite young. Used to throw a tantrum. We mostly didn't bother; it wasn't worth the trouble. I remember at Karen's wedding – Beth was supposed to be a bridesmaid. We bought all the bridesmaids pretty dresses. Beth absolutely refused to wear hers. She had a terrible row with Phil. And she wouldn't be in the wedding pictures.

"There was one... we gave it to the police. But I think we got it back. I'll have a look."

She went out of the room and returned carrying a photo. It was the original of the one printed in the *Gazette*. It was better quality, and in colour.

"This is the only picture of Beth. Somebody took it without her seeing – she never knew about it. She doesn't look very good in it – a funny look on her face."

"Would you mind if I took a picture of this with my phone?"

"I suppose not."

Yolanda took a couple of shots and handed the picture back.

"Thank you very much for your time, Mrs Winthrop, it was good of you to answer all these questions."

Yolanda pointed at the photos on the coffee table.

"You have a lovely family."

Mrs Winthrop beamed.

◆ ◆ ◆

Driving home, Yolanda thought about everything Linda Winthrop had said. Especially the bombshell she'd dropped at the end. Beth had actually written a letter two months after she went missing. That must be the final piece of the jigsaw. She'd met someone – no doubt someone her parents wouldn't approve of – and gone off with him. Yolanda had too many questions. Even ten years ago, everyone had phones, why a letter and not a phone call? What girl of that age wrote letters? Linda recognised the handwriting, but letters could be forged, handwriting copied. Or the letter could've been written under duress. Receiving a letter like that with some critical, nasty remarks about the family would be a good way to stop them trying to find Beth. Giving up on her for good.

As soon as Yolanda got home, she looked at the photo of Beth on her phone, making it as large as possible. Finally, she could really see what the girl looked like. She stood in front of the portrait on the wall, holding up her phone. Margery had certainly captured Beth's expression. By exaggerating the size and darkness of her eyes against the pale skin of her face, Margery had intensified the girl's emotion. In fact, Beth's eyes were a light hazel colour, whereas in the portrait they looked almost black.

Now she appreciated the true colour of Beth's abundant hair – somewhere between red and blonde, it was lighter than in the portrait. As several people had described, the hair hung either side of Beth's face, its weight pulling down the curls into waves.

As Yolanda examined the photo, there was something familiar about it. Something she recognised. Then she recalled Linda Winthrop, with her faded auburn hair and pale skin. Of course, that must be the resemblance. Beth favoured her mother.

◆ ◆ ◆

Yolanda's phone rang. She saw with a sinking heart it was Jackie.

"Hi Mum."

"Hello Yolanda. What's going on – George tells me you're still away?

"I just stayed on a few more days, my trial got cancelled. I had some leave owing, it's no big deal."

"If your trial got cancelled does that mean you've got no other work? Does everyone just take time off and go on holiday?"

"No, but..."

"Is there any rule that says you've got to take all your leave? Do they force you to take it?"

"No, of course not."

"I don't understand you. Did you ever see me take time off? No – not if there was work to be done, and there was always work to be done."

Yolanda said nothing

"You've seen how hard I worked. I had no university education, no help, no money. All I had was drive and ambition. I had to make it for you, for us. You don't know how lucky you are. You're clever, you had every encouragement. The best of everything. Top university, all the clothes you need."

"I know, Mum and I appreciate..."

"You have a wonderful opportunity. A job like that with a top London firm – the sky's the limit. I can't bear to see you throw it away."

"Mum, I'm not throwing anything away, I just took a few days off for a break and to focus on my art..."

"Your art... What're you talking about? You're a lawyer. Why're you wasting your time on art? How many times have I told you, in a firm like yours, everybody's ready to stab you in the back, push you out. They'll walk all over you to get to the top. If you show weakness or you're not motivated, you're finished. I told you, make yourself indispensable to them – it's the only way. Don't kid yourself, there're plenty of hot shot lawyers just as good as you. You don't get to the top by being better than the others, you get there by wanting it more and working harder. And this sort of thing, taking weeks off work, shows them you don't want it."

Now Yolanda was crying, she couldn't speak. Jackie was still in full flow.

"I'm always on the lookout for new opportunities – even now I've got ideas. I'm going after something big... something I've always wanted.

"I'm disappointed in you. You've let me down. I expected more. What's really going on down there? What's wrong with you? Are you pregnant?"

"No," she moaned, "Mum, please,"

"I can't speak to you anymore. I'm too upset."

Yolanda sat down on the sofa. Jackie'd never spoken to her like that before. She'd certainly reprimanded her daughter, always voicing her views as if they were absolute truths. Yolanda had always found it easier to keep quiet and never challenged her mum. This outpouring of anger had left her shaking. She kept hearing her mum's words; 'I'm disappointed in you. You've let me down. I expected more.' Although she'd never said so, Yolanda knew her mum was proud of her. But now... She sat in the dark, weeping uncontrollably.

Her phone rang. She saw it was Robin and didn't answer. A few minutes later it rang again.

"Hi, it's Robin. How're you? We're at the pub and wondered if you're coming?'

"No, I'm not, I'm not in the mood."

"What's wrong? Your voice sounds... Are you ill?"

"No, I'm fine," said Yolanda, her voice thick with tears.

"I can tell you're not fine, what's wrong? I only want to help."

At these words, Yolanda dissolved into tears again.

"It's really nothing," she said between sobs, "it's stupid, I just had a phone call with my mum..."

"I'm coming round now, is that okay, can I come?"

"If you want to, but..."

"I'll be with you soon."

◆ ◆ ◆

Yolanda stood up. She turned on the light, washed her face and brushed her hair. She was tidying the living room when Robin arrived. She opened the door and Robin stood there, carrying a bag.

"How're you feeling?"

"Much better. It's so kind of you to come."

"Have you eaten?"

Yolanda frowned.

"I can't remember. I don't think so."

"I thought not. I brought some soup; it'll only take a few minutes to heat up."

They were soon sitting at the table, with bowls of soup and cheese scones – slightly stale but still tasty.

"This soup's delicious, what flavour is it? Where did you get it?"

"Leek and potato. I made it. It's really easy, I love making soup."

"I used to like cooking," said Yolanda, "could you send me the recipe?"

"Of course."

They finished the food in companionable silence. Robin pushed her bowl away.

"Do you want to talk about..."

Yolanda shrugged.

"There's nothing much to say. My mum doesn't agree with my lifestyle and choices. She told me so in no uncertain terms. I dare say she's right. But she's never been so angry before. She said some things... It's ridiculous, it shouldn't affect me. I deal with difficult clients all the time."

"It's different when it's your mum."

"Yes. I suppose it hasn't happened before, because I've done everything she wanted. I didn't always agree, but..."

"What was she upset about?"

"About me taking so much time off work, coming down here. Then I made the mistake of mentioning my art. She doesn't believe in hobbies. She doesn't believe in anything apart from working and making money. She thinks I should be like her.

"To be fair, she's done very well, building her business up from scratch. She was a single parent and did it all herself. She knows how hard life can be and doesn't want that for me. In her opinion I'm throwing away my chances of success."

"What does success mean to you?"

"To be honest, I don't know anymore. I used to think I wanted the same as Mum. Actually, that's not true, I didn't think about it at all. I just kept on going down the road that stretched ahead of me, school, university. I never questioned whether that was the path – or the end result – I wanted.

"I think the change started with the art class I joined. They were nice – friendly, supportive. I realised that even outside work, all the people I socialised with weren't real friends. When I was with them, I was still on duty, on guard, just the same as at work. Keeping up with them, feeling judged by them all the time.

"Then when I came down here and met you and the others, I saw there were alternatives. I met people who had different values. Money wasn't everything. My lifestyle's been expensive: takeaways, cocktails, shots. I could live happily on much less, in the right place, with the right friends."

"Wow," said Robin, "that's a lot to think about."

Yolanda noticed the time.

"I'm so sorry, it's late and you've got work tomorrow."

"That's okay. But perhaps we should call it a night. How do you feel?"

"I have a lot of questions, but I feel much better. I'll go to the beach tomorrow to try and work out some answers."

CHAPTER 7

The next day the good weather returned. Sunshine poured into the bedroom and Yolanda took her time getting up. She was pottering around the flat, when her phone rang. It was Robin.

"Good morning, I hope this isn't too early?"

"Of course not."

"How're you feeling?"

"Surprisingly well."

"Would you like to come over to me this evening for a bite?"

"I'd love that."

"It won't be anything fancy. See you about six thirty?"

"Great."

Yolanda had never had a friend like Robin before – someone with whom she could let down her guard, express her feelings without censoring them. Robin genuinely cared about people and wanted to help them. Perhaps Yolanda hadn't let anyone get close because she'd always suspected their motives, assumed they had an angle. If she'd opened up more, she might've made friends like Robin before. It was very liberating to discuss her problems with someone sympathetic, like she used to with Tony. What a shame she'd lost touch with him. She must look him up the next time she went to see her mum.

Yolanda wandered down to the beach with her sketchbook. She sat outside Pav's with a cup of coffee, luxuriating in the sun. There were few people around. It was hard to imagine this beach crowded, but it must be in the summer. She opened her sketchbook. Too lazy to draw, she flipped through the pages. She came to the flowers she'd drawn at the art group meeting. That seemed ages ago. So much had happened since. They were nice pictures, but she'd moved on.

"They're really good," said a voice, "are you an artist?"

The young girl wiping the tables looked as if she should've been at school. Yolanda smiled.

"Have you been to the sunken garden, there're lots of flowers there you can draw?" said the girl.

"Where's that?"

"You go past the tennis courts over there," said the helpful young lady.

Intrigued, Yolanda made her way over the grassy cliff. She saw the tennis courts, and envisioned herself playing a game after work, or having a picnic on the beach. The notion was intoxicating. She reached the rectangular garden and climbed down the few steps. It was a quiet, sheltered place with a profusion of flowers in delicate colours. A haven. She sat on a bench and breathed out. It seemed as if all the air kept pent up in her lungs for years was released. She shut her eyes.

She blinked. She must've been dozing. It was nearly lunchtime. She felt like cooking pasta. At the deli, she bought olives and mozzarella. At an old-fashioned greengrocers, she bought tomatoes, lettuce and cucumber. It would be nice to take something to Robin, she could make a fruit salad.

Back in the flat, Yolanda googled a recipe and half an hour later she was eating a bowl of pasta on the balcony. This was the life, who needed the Mediterranean?

Sitting in the sun, she looked up the Law Society website on her phone. She scrolled to the section listing vacancies for solicitors and searched under East Kent.

◆ ◆ ◆

Yolanda rang Robin's doorbell, and handed over a covered dish.

"My contribution. Fruit salad."

"You didn't need to..."

"Preparing food's quite soothing, I enjoy it. I'd forgotten."

While they were eating, Yolanda brought Robin up to date on what she'd found out from James Perrot.

"It was interesting to meet him."

"What happened with Amber?"

"I knew most of the facts, but I got a picture of the two girls' characters – specially Amber's. And also, their relationship. They were quite different, opposites, and quickly fell out. The most surprising thing happened right at the end – she was a bit tipsy by then, and let out more than she meant to."

Yolanda repeated Amber's words about Beth and described the expression on her face.

"You don't think Amber hated Beth enough to… hurt her?"

"She could hardly have killed her and hidden the body – that's too far-fetched. But I can't forget the look on her face."

Yolanda grimaced.

"The meal cost me a fortune, I told her the newspaper was paying and I encouraged her to have quite a bit to drink."

"Did you see Beth's parents?"

"I saw her mum, and that was useful – it was conclusive."

She recounted the conversation. When she came to the part about the letter from Beth, after her disappearance, Robin gasped.

"Was she sure the letter really was from Beth?"

"That's what I asked, but she was adamant it was her handwriting."

"Why write a letter and not phone?" said Robin, screwing up her face, "that sounds odd."

"Yes, and she was hiding something about the letter. I couldn't work out what."

"Did you see it?

"No, she said she'd torn it up."

"I don't see what more you can do."

"Neither do I."

Yolanda noticed the time.

"Are we going to the pub?"

"Yes, if you feel like it."

"Of course."

◆ ◆ ◆

They were the first ones to arrive at the pub. Pete came next and sat down beside Yolanda. He was wearing a tweed waistcoat over a black polo neck and a hat as usual. She wondered what he'd look like without it. He was probably losing his hair like Andy and was sensitive. Tash, Melody and Andy soon arrived.

"No choir tonight, Tash?" asked Robin.

"No, Marion's on holiday. By the way, I'm off to Hatfield next week, for the big craft fair. I can't wait."

"That's one of the best in the country," said Melody, "I had a stall there one year to sell my cards, but it was so expensive, I didn't make much. You can't charge a lot for cards, so the smaller fairs are better."

"There're a couple of fairs in London with top jewellery makers," said Pete, "I couldn't afford a stall, but it's good to visit – you can pick up all sorts of ideas."

"I'm going to Comic Con," Andy said, "that's also next month, in London. I'm going to crash at my friend's pad."

"What's Comic Con?" said Yolanda.

Robin groaned.

"Don't get him started."

"You guys go on about craft fairs, why can't I talk about Comic Con?"

"I'm interested," said Yolanda, "I've never heard about craft fairs or Comic Con before."

"It's great," said Andy, "it's held in a big venue – loads of comics for sale, fan artwork, you get to meet the artists. I'm hoping to meet some agents and pitch my graphic novel idea. And I can get together with friends I haven't seen for ages. Have a look at these photos from last year's Comic Con. Here Pete, pass it over to her."

Yolanda took the phone from Pete, and as their hands touched, she felt a shock that was almost electric.

"I've lived in London for years," she said, looking at the photos, "but I've clearly been missing out."

"You can come with us, if you like," said Andy, "it's more fun to go in a group."

"Bunch of geeks," said Robin, but she was smiling.

"I might take you up on that." said Yolanda.

"Do you like living in London?" Pete asked.

"I've lived there for more than ten years, but haven't really taken advantage of it. I've only started going to galleries and museums in the last year, my art teacher's been suggesting places."

"You must find it much quieter down here," Pete went on.

"It is quiet. It's given me a chance to think about things."

"What've you been up to, apart from thinking?"

"I've been trying to solve... something." she said, staring into the distance. "Somebody disappeared."

She was silent, still perplexed by the case.

◆ ◆ ◆

The next day it was cloudy, but rain wasn't forecast. Yolanda ate her muesli on the balcony, and gazed at the sea which reflected the grey skies. She thought about Beth. Even though the puzzle seemed to be solved, the ending wasn't satisfying. What was the song Beth had requested from James? What was it called? 'Now Is the Time.'

On YouTube she found two versions, neither with many views. Clearly it wasn't popular. She played the first – a middle aged man singing in his bedroom. The sound was poor. She tried the other. This featured a couple of teenagers performing on a school stage. The sound quality was better, and the tune was quite catchy, but Yolanda couldn't make out the words properly. Google provided the full lyrics.

Now is the time to stop pretending

To say what is true.

Now is the time to start defending

The real you.

Now is the time to start embracing

The essence of your soul.

Now is the time to start replacing

That worn out goal.

Now is the time to stop conforming

To other people's rules.

Now is the time to start transforming
With your own set of tools.

Now is the time to study your reflection
To stand and stare.
Now is the time to change direction
If you dare.

What did this mean to Beth?

◆ ◆ ◆

Yolanda couldn't let go of the mystery. She decided to go to Broadstairs – she hadn't seen it in the daylight – and visit places Beth had been. She stopped on the outskirts of the town, by the school field which was used as the Folk Week campsite. She got out of the car, but there was nothing to see. According to the Folk Week website, it was a fifteen to twenty-minute walk to the centre of town. Yolanda left her car outside the school to retrace Beth's steps. She passed a couple of pubs on her way, which hosted events during Folk Week. On this grey day it was hard to imagine the streets full of suntanned folk fans in holiday mood.

The Broadstairs streets were lined with interesting shops, seaside takeaways and cafes. She hadn't yet reached the sea. A sign with an arrow pointed to a cafe and she followed it, surprised to find herself entering a hotel. The Royal Albion. The receptionist directed her through the lounge to the cafe. This had glass doors to a terrace. As Yolanda pushed open the glass door, the sun came out. This wasn't what she expected. She stepped out onto a raised terrace with a sweeping view of the wide, sandy bay. A few of the outside tables were occupied and Yolanda sat down. How surprising, what a magnificent panorama. The elevated terrace was the perfect place to take it in. Now the sun sparkled on the sea. The latte was average, but the setting wasn't. Yolanda relaxed into the warmth of the sun. She thought of Beth.

She brought up the lyrics of the song on her phone and read them again. Maybe there was something she'd missed, a clue to Beth's fascination with the song. Written out like this, it read like a poem. The theme was of introspection, self-examination. The reader (or listener) was urged to search deep within to find her authentic self, her true values, needs and goals. The call to action was urgent and powerful. The reader must change their outlook, habits, way of living, to align with this knowledge.

Beth had chosen to listen to the song over and over again, perhaps the words had given her the insight and will to do something about her own situation. Her poor relationship with her family, lack of friends and dead-end jobs. Either she'd gone over to France as the police thought, or somewhere else in Britain. For a fresh start. This made sense. It was the most likely explanation for Beth's disappearance. Trying to look further would be pointless, but still...

Yolanda studied the song, line by line, word by word, as if it were a legal document.

Stop pretending

Say what is true.

Did this resonate with Beth? How had she been pretending? Why? Was it shame? Guilt? To protect herself or someone else? To hide a secret? Yolanda's heart beat faster. Her chest tightened. This was dangerous ground. She recoiled, but the word was there. Abuse.

That would explain Beth's unhappiness, her difficulties. Her anguished expression in the picture. Had Beth been abused? Did the song give her the strength to finally take action...? Yolanda gasped. What if Beth had confronted her abuser and he silenced her?

"May I clear away, Madam? Is there anything else I can get you?"

Yolanda started. She looked round the terrace, the tables were filling up and she'd have to order something if she wanted to keep this prime position.

"Another latte, please."

She tried to banish the horrific ideas. Further investigation could wait. She took a deep breath and sat back in the sun, but it didn't work. She couldn't escape from her thoughts about Beth. The idea must be faced. Linda Winthrop's description of her daughter's behaviour could be consistent with abuse.... But who was the abuser? There were a couple of obvious possibilities. Beth's father Phil. He seemed the likeliest – because of his proximity and his attitude towards the girl. Linda described how twice she wanted Beth to see a professional therapist or counsellor, but Phil refused. That was suspicious. Wouldn't any father want help for his child? But Phil was disturbed by misfits, freaks and weirdos, maybe he just didn't want to have Beth labelled as one of these.

His relationship with Beth didn't sound ideal, but she remembered he did take his daughter to swimming training regularly. Could something have happened then? She blocked out the scene, she couldn't bear to think of the details.

Swimming training suggested another alternative. Beth's coach. The coach of a young girl was in a position of trust. This trust could be abused, especially with a vulnerable girl like Beth. Linda said Beth had suddenly turned against swimming, refused to even get in the water. Could this be a reaction to inappropriate behaviour by her coach? Such a situation could leave Beth traumatised and lead to her later problems. On the other hand, she had problems before she began swimming training, these couldn't all be attributed to the coach.

The only other potential abuser that Yolanda was aware of, was Beth's brother, Brett. She recalled the photo on Linda's coffee table, of the tall teenager. He was quite a bit older than Beth.

Of course, there may've been other possibilities, a neighbour, friend of the family, teacher. What could Yolanda do with this new idea? Was there any way to follow it up? Today was Friday and she was returning to London on Sunday. She only had the Saturday.

She could return to the Winthrop family home to speak to Beth's father, Phil, but from Linda's account, he sounded irascible, and likely to give her short shrift if she tried to ask about Beth or her disappearance. Beth's swimming coach from fifteen years earlier would be impossible to trace. That left Brett, Beth's brother. He was probably the least likely to be the abuser, but the easiest to approach. Linda said he had an optician's shop in Chelmsford. Yolanda checked online and from the General Optical Council's register of opticians, she found Brett's shop. She phoned to try and arrange an eye test for the following day, without much hope.

"I'm afraid Mr Winthrop's fully booked for tomorrow. He could manage next Saturday, if that's any good to you?"

Yolanda sighed. Once she was back in London, she wouldn't have time for any of this.

"Is there any way I could see him privately, I'm quite willing to pay?"

"Please hold on a minute," said the polite receptionist. After a pause she came back. "Could you get here early, say eight thirty?"

"Yes, that would be okay."

"Mr Winthrop's first appointment's at nine and he's always in early. If you're here by eight thirty, you can see him."

It was as simple as that.

◆ ◆ ◆

After she made the appointment, Yolanda's phone rang, it was Robin.

“Hi, do you fancy going to see a film tonight? There's something good on – *Me Before You.*”

“Yes, sure. What about the others?”

“I'm going to call them. I'll have to tell Andy it's got a car chase. It's on in Westgate. Meet outside the cinema at seven thirty? We can go to the Swan after for a drink, it’s just around the corner.”

“Do you need a lift?”

“No thanks, I'll have the car. See you later.”

Yolanda walked to the cinema. It was a strange-looking building in the High Street. Tash was outside and greeted her with a grin.

“What do you think of the building?”

“I'm not sure. Was it always a cinema, it looks more like a castle?”

“No, originally it was the town hall. Westgate was very grand in those days. Looked down on Margate and Ramsgate. They built a town hall based on one in Switzerland.”

“It's the most unusual cinema I’ve ever seen.”

Soon the others turned up.

“You're sure there's at least one car chase?” Andy was saying as they went inside.

◆ ◆ ◆

After the film they sat in the Swan.

“What did you think of it?” asked Robin.

“For a film about euthanasia, it was surprisingly entertaining,” said Andy, “but I'm still waiting for the car chase.”

“Yes, sorry about that,” said Robin, “I’ll buy you a bag of crisps to make up for it.”

“Now you're talking, I'd forgive anything for a bag of crisps – as long as they’re salt and vinegar.”

“I didn't like the ending,” said Tash, “I really thought he’d change his mind in the end, and not go through with it.”

“I thought it was good – true to life. There aren’t many happy endings in real life,” said Melody.

“What do you think, Yolanda?” said Robin.

“Money doesn't solve all problems. However much money he had – he still couldn't walk and do the things he used to.”

“But it helps,” said Melody, “he had all those facilities and he could afford an easy death. What do you think, Pete?”

“It reminded me; however bad your problems seem; there’re other people with worse.”

Yolanda wondered what Pete's problems were.

“My problem is I'm still waiting for the crisps,” said Andy pulling a sad face. They all laughed and Robin went to the bar. She threw the bag across the table to Andy.

“I don't like encouraging you to eat unhealthy food.”

“Are crisps unhealthy?” said Andy, “I thought they were potatoes – like, you know, vegetables.”

“What’ve you been doing today?” Pete asked Yolanda, “More thinking?”

She smiled.

“Yes, actually I have.”

“Come to any conclusions?”

“Only that Broadstairs Bay is magnificent.”

“I wouldn't argue with that.”

“I've also been… retracing steps.”

“That sounds mysterious, whose steps?”

Yolanda spoke slowly, looking down at the melting ice in her drink.

"A girl. A girl who disappeared a long time ago. I've been wondering how she felt. Trying to understand her.

What've you been up to?" She asked Pete, but he didn't reply. She looked up. He was staring into the distance.

Melody noticed the exchange.

"He isn't listening, he's probably wondering if he remembered to lock the car."

"Or if he left the iron or oven on." added Tash.

"I'm always leaving the oven on," said Andy, "I get an idea for the book, start drawing and the next thing I know there's a smell of burning and the pizza's dead. I don't own an iron."

"That's obvious," said Robin.

"When're you going back to London, Yolanda?" asked Andy.

"On Sunday. So, I probably won't see you again for a while."

"Comic Con's next weekend – are you coming?"

"Yes, I'd like to, can we arrange to meet?"

"I'll give you a call the day before."

"Yolanda," said Tash, "I hope you'll come down here the week after – it's my birthday on the Sunday and I'm having a party. A barbecue. Everyone's invited."

"I'd love to come," said Yolanda and Robin said immediately.

"You can stay with me; we've got plenty of room."

"Lucky it's not the same day as the Comic Con," said Andy, "I wouldn't know which one to go to." They all laughed.

◆ ◆ ◆

On Saturday morning, Yolanda was taking no chances and arrived early at the optician's shop in Chelmsford. It was in a prime location. In the window, an attractive range of spectacle frames – from exotic designer brands to the utilitarian end of the market were displayed. The door was locked, but several members of staff were visible inside.

The door was opened just before eight thirty. The receptionist smiled at Yolanda.

“Mr Winthrop’s ready for you, come straight through, please.”

Brett stood up to greet her. He was tall, with grey hair – although he couldn't have been more than forty. He had broad shoulders and a firm handshake.

“Any special reason for the test?” he asked.

Yolanda had prepared for this.

“My eyes get sore when I've been working on the computer all day. I wondered if I've got eye strain – need glasses.”

She had, in fact, experienced these symptoms and been given drops by her doctor.

Brett carried out the test with minimal conversation. She took a chance.

“Are you any relation to Linda Winthrop?”

Brett continued to manipulate lenses, and spoke without interest.

“Yes, she’s my mother.”

“My friend, her name's Amber, she knows your sister. Does she still live in Chelmsford?”

“Karen? Yes, she does.

“Now I'm just going to put drops in your eyes. Look up please.”

“No, not Karen, Beth.”

Brett dropped the bottle on the floor, and a dark stain spread across the carpet. He bent down.

“I do apologise, I’ll get a new bottle. Please excuse me.” Brett was flustered on his return and his hands shook as he inserted the drops.

"Please take a seat outside, the drops will take a few minutes to work."

Yolanda left the room, but as she shut the door she looked back. Brett was sitting, his head in his hands. The mention of Beth had upset him. How to make the most of this opportunity? She thought rapidly.

Brett checked her eyes in silence, but ignoring his discomfiture, she spoke.

"Did you say Beth still lives in Chelmsford? My friend hasn't mentioned her lately."

Forced to reply, Brett stammered.

"My sister, er, Beth, she hasn't lived in the area for a long time. She, er, went away. We're not in touch."

He pulled himself together.

"Your eyes look fine to me. No sign of eye strain. The soreness is probably due to a lack of lubrication. I'll give some drops. They're a harmless saline solution. Use them as often as you need."

He stood up, anxious to get away.

"Thank you so much for fitting me in at such short notice, Mr Winthrop. Really kind. And you put my mind at rest. I'll definitely use the drops."

Brett almost pushed Yolanda out of the room.

"My receptionist will deal with the payment..."

Beads of sweat stood out on the man's forehead.

Yolanda wondered what to do next, it was still early – not even half past nine. She could try Beth's home. She parked a short distance from the house and sat in the car. This was a wild goose chase. She wasn't going to knock on the door, she might as well go back to Westgate.

Yolanda started the engine and took a last look at Beth's house. The door opened and someone came out. Two people actually, a tall man with white hair, holding the hand of a boy of three or four. The man shut the door, and the pair walked down the drive to the road. They turned right. Their pace was slow, as the child stopped frequently, looking up at the man and pointing at things along the way. This must be Phil and his grandson, one of Brett's or Karen's children. They were out for a Saturday morning walk.

From the car, Yolanda watched them. How could she approach them? She racked her brains. Then the miracle happened. A tiny miracle, but a miracle, nonetheless. The child dropped something. It was small and red, but Yolanda couldn't make out what it was. She held her breath, would the grandfather notice? He didn't. Neither of them looked back.

Yolanda watched their progress anxiously and when they were far enough away not to notice her, got out of the car. She picked up the red object – it was a small woollen hat – and followed the pair, keeping her distance.

They continued along the road and then turned into the entrance of a park. She followed them. There were few other people around. She hurried up to the pair.

"Excuse me, I think you dropped this."

She held out the hat with a smile.

"Is this yours, Jake?" the man asked the boy.

"Yes, it's my winter hat. It's in my pocket."

"Well, it isn't now, it fell out and this nice lady found it. Thank you for spotting it. What do you say, Jake?"

"Thank you. Can I go on the slide now, Grandad?"

"Alright, off you go. They're always losing things at that age," said the man, gazing fondly at the small figure. "My name's Phil Winthrop. He's my grandson." There was pride in his voice.

"I'm Yolanda Blake."

They sat down on a bench.

"He's a nice-looking boy, how old is he?"

That sounded the right thing to say.

"He's a good lad, though I say so myself. He'll be four soon. They grow up so fast."

"How many grandchildren do you have?"

"My daughter's got two – they're older. Jake is Brett – my son's – youngest. He's got three."

"Grandad! Watch!" The boy shouted and waved from the top of the slide.

Phil waved back. When the boy landed safely, he ran to the bench.

"Grandad, can I have some sweets?"

"Now Jake, what makes you think I've got sweets?"

"You've always got sweets, Grandad," he put his small hand in Phil's pocket. "Here they are!" A packet of sweets was drawn out in triumph. "Can I have them?"

Phil stroked the child's hair.

"All of them?" he asked in mock surprise.

"Yes," said the boy, "but I'll give the nice lady one."

Yolanda took the sticky offering. Phil chuckled and the boy ran off.

"I know I spoil them. But they're such a joy, kids. You've got to make the most of them."

"My mum wouldn't agree," the words had slipped out before Yolanda could stop them, "she thinks children are a burden."

What was the matter with her? Why was she saying this? To him?

Phil's brow furrowed and he shook his head.

"I wasn't so good with my own kids. Wasn't a good dad. I was hard on them."

Yolanda sat still. What'd she started?

"You were hard on them?"

"Yes, especially the youngest. I didn't understand. I thought I was doing the right thing – being tough for her own good. But I see now I was wrong."

"My mum was hard on me. She still is. She still wants to control me."

Phil nodded.

"I know that feeling. You think you know what's best for them – if they'd only do what you say... You get angry. But it doesn't work, you just turn them against you. Make them miserable. Your mum doesn't mean it. She wants to do the best for you, even if it doesn't seem like that."

She wasn't sure he was right. He went on,

"Then something happened. She... my daughter went away. Wrote a letter saying we were cruel to her, didn't understand her, didn't even try to. She was so miserable, she never wanted to see us again."

Yolanda said nothing. She felt guilty, she was deceiving Phil, tricking him, but she had to hear more about Beth.

"It was a terrible time. The worst time of my life."

She had to say something.

"I'm sorry."

"Ten years ago, now, but it seems much less. We – all the family – felt so guilty. I knew it was my fault – everything she said was true. I was so hard on her. I never thought about her side of things. That she was suffering, couldn't help herself. I wasn't kind. Always shouting. That didn't help."

He stared into the distance, ignoring his grandson's calls. The boy ran up.

"Grandad, you're not looking at me! Watch me this time!"

The man nodded and stroked the boy's cheek.

"My son – this one's dad – he thought it was his fault, he used to tease her, you know like big brothers do, thought it was a joke. But when she went, he was so upset. Even now, if he hears her name... He's a big fellow, but he just goes to pieces. My wife and other daughter as well – you never get over something like that. Knowing you've driven your own child away. I was so sorry. I hoped she'd come back, sometime… So I could tell her. Make it up to her." Tears glistened in his eyes.

"Mr Winthrop," said Yolanda, with a catch in her voice, "don't give up hope. Your daughter may well come back... She may not be ready yet. But one day..."

This man was not an abuser, Yolanda would've staked her life on it.

CHAPTER 8

On Sunday morning Yolanda packed her bags and went round the flat to make sure she hadn't forgotten anything. She took a lingering look at the painting of Beth. It was hard to leave. So much had happened, she couldn't believe it was only a fortnight before that she'd arrived. She locked the front door after her and posted the key through the letterbox. And that was that.

◆ ◆ ◆

Back in London she spent the day catching up on two weeks' worth of chores and getting ready for work. Going into the office on Monday morning, she felt as if she'd been away for a long time.

“The wanderer returns,” said Harvey, “I'm surprised you can still find this place.”

She ignored him. Two of her female colleagues – ‘friends’ she went out drinking with – stared at her wavy hair.

“Cool hairstyle, Yolanda,” and then she caught in a lower tone, “must be a new trend. I'd kill for that look.”

She smiled, back to normal.

Gareth, the team leader, stopped by her desk.

“Yolanda, there's something we need to talk about. My office at twelve thirty."

Harvey didn't miss this. He came over.

"Your little trip didn't escape Gareth's eagle eye. Now you're for it." he drew his finger across his throat with an unpleasant smile.

Yolanda couldn't help feeling anxious when she entered Gareth's office.

"Let's get out of here," he said, "we can talk over a drink." In the bar, Gareth ordered a double whisky for himself and Yolanda asked for soda water.

"Your work hasn't gone unnoticed." Gareth said, "That settlement wouldn't have happened without your input. The partners have their eye on you and they're pleased with what they see. I'd like you to take on more cases like that in the future, so I'll be putting your name forward for promotion. Harvey's going to be upset – he's a big talker and he thought he was in line for this. I can see through him. But you've impressed me. I believe in recognising and rewarding real merit and hard work."

Gareth's words surprised Yolanda, she thought he was taken in by Harvey's sycophantic behaviour and encouraged it. The team leader rose in her estimation. His recognition and support could make a big difference to her future in the firm.

"It'll mean a serious pay rise." Gareth continued.

When he mentioned the figure, she was stunned. He smiled at her expression.

"It shows what we think of you. This is just the first step, you're on your way to the top. You might treat yourself to a new car, a nice trip."

Yolanda thanked him. The sum Gareth spoke of was significant, it changed everything. She had a lot to think about. The possibilities unlocked by his words dazzled her. The glowing terms in which he described her abilities and future made her think.

In this frame of mind, anything was possible. She could become a team leader, even a partner in the firm. Then she could influence the ethos and atmosphere, make it more harmonious. She pictured herself in a large office, handling the most important and interesting cases, yet still finding time to mentor and encourage others.

The attractions of living in Westgate faded. She could always go down for weekends. Rent the Airbnb again. She could buy a bigger flat in London, and Robin and the others could come and stay. In time she could buy a holiday home down there.

This pleasant reverie was interrupted by the ringing of her phone. It was her mum. They hadn't spoken since Jackie's rant when Yolanda was in Westgate. The subject was still on her mum's mind.

"Are you back at work now? I hope there won't be any repercussions. You'll have to put in some overtime – do something to impress them."

Yolanda's anger rose.

"I've obviously done something to impress them, I've just been told I'm in line for promotion."

"How much'll you be getting?" Jackie asked.

Yolanda was immediately sorry she'd brought this up. She wanted time to think over the matter before sharing any more with her mum.

"I don't know the details and it's not definite."

"Don't count your chickens. They can promise anything – unless it's in writing it's meaningless. Well, you were lucky. You got away with it this time. But the higher you get the harder you need to work. Get rid of this idea that you must take all your leave. It shows you're not really committed. Don't swan off like that again."

Yolanda's heart was pounding. Jackie's remarks infuriated her.

Why does she always tell me what to do? Jackie's unsolicited advice irked her more than usual. I'll show her, I'll become a partner. Then she'll have to stop. She'll understand I know what I'm doing. Even while she was telling herself this, the realisation dawned. Jackie would never stop. No matter how high she rose, Jackie would never trust her. She would always interfere and try to control Yolanda's life.

◆ ◆ ◆

On the Wednesday, Yolanda went to her art class. The teacher was impressed by the work she'd done. She told Claudia about Comic Con.

"Can I come?" Claudia asked, "Joseph would love that."

Yolanda spoke to Robin several times and exchanged messages with Andy about Comic Con.

◆ ◆ ◆

On Friday morning, Gareth stopped Yolanda in the corridor.

"You haven't been to the bar this week, we've missed you. But you must come tonight, two of the senior partners will be there – I want to make the case for your promotion. And not the usual place – the Luna instead."

When Yolanda entered the bar, Gareth came over to her. He was flushed and she recoiled from the whisky fumes on his breath.

"Here's the rising star, glad you came."

She looked around but saw nobody else from the firm.

"Hi, Gareth, where're the others? Didn't you say the senior partners would be here?"

He smiled. "There's been a bit of a mix up – it's just you and me. Come and sit down. What're you drinking?"

"Just soda water please."

He led her over to a dark corner. When he went off to the bar, Yolanda gathered her wits. Something was going on. She'd got to work with this guy, she'd better be careful not to offend him. Gareth set down a glass in front of her. He moved closer, his breath making her gasp.

"Perhaps it's not such a bad thing the others didn't turn up, we can go into more details about your promotion." He grinned. "Had any thoughts about the new car? When you're young and free you can go for something special – make the others jealous – specially Harvey," he laughed too loudly. "Maybe we can get you a bigger office, how'd you like that? Closer to me." he nudged her. "More convenient."

He edged closer to her and Yolanda leant back.

"Drink up." he said, "Once you're in the new job, with all that lovely money, we'll be having more meetings, you and me."

Gareth's leg was pressed against hers. There was no mistaking his intention. Her thoughts raced. How to get away without offending him? He took her hand.

"This is cosy. How about you and me making a night of it?"

How about your wife, Yolanda was tempted to reply? But she retrieved her hand, looked him in the face and spoke in a calm, even voice.

"Sorry Gareth, I've got an arrangement with friends. They're expecting me."

"Why don't you ring and cancel? We can go wherever you like – top hotel – money no object."

"I'm afraid that's not possible."

In spite of a pounding heart, Yolanda sat still, to indicate she'd nothing more to say. Gareth's face was now scarlet, with the petulant expression of a spoilt child who'd been denied a treat.

"That's not very helpful. If I recommend someone for promotion, I expect them to be more – obliging."

She said nothing.

"If you don't want to cooperate, you can forget about the promotion," he said and watched for her reaction.

"Then I'll have to bear the disappointment."

He looked at her sharply, suspecting she was making fun of him. But her expression was inscrutable.

"Good evening," she said, standing up. "Thanks for the drink." she strode away, leaving her glass untouched.

Yolanda walked calmly out of the bar. Only outside did she begin to shake. The streets were crowded with homeward-bound commuters and revellers starting their weekend. As she walked to the station, everything around her was a discordant, intrusive blur. She shrank into herself, keeping her elbows out to avoid being jostled.

Her mind numb, she automatically passed through the station onto the platform. Masses of remorseless humanity were everywhere. The train roared in, throwing out a blast of heat. Once again, the stench of Gareth's breath was in her nostrils and her head swam. Yolanda clutched the back of a bench. She let the train go.

Once the air had cooled, she took a couple of deep breaths and felt better. The next train arrived quickly, but was full. She hung onto a handle, helplessly swaying with the motion, and fought down the nausea that rose in her stomach. Reaching each station without throwing up was an achievement. Finally, she got out at West Hampstead and breathed deeply. The queasiness subsided.

Yolanda slowly climbed the stairs into the street. Here too, herds of people thronged the main road. The sky was beginning to darken, making the lights of the cafes, restaurants and bars all the more garish. She'd never realised how many cuisines were represented on her way home. Curry, pizza, fried chicken and a myriad of oriental and Middle Eastern aromas assaulted Yolanda with competing aromas.

At last, she was home. She shut the door and locked it. Shivering from shock and exhaustion, she went into the bathroom, stripped off all her clothes and stepped into a scalding shower. She washed her body and hair over and over again. Only then did the shaking stop. In pyjamas and dressing gown she sat huddled on the sofa with a mug of tea, wrapped in a blanket. She'd never felt so alone.

◆ ◆ ◆

Yolanda slept badly and awoke feeling fragile. She forced herself to carry on with her usual Saturday morning routine. She put on laundry, cleaned the flat and did the ironing. Thoughts of the encounter with Gareth picked at the edges of her mind, while she tried to focus on the mundane tasks. But it had to be faced sometime. She sat on the sofa with a cup of tea and considered the incident. She'd escaped last night but shuddered at the memory and the thought of working for Gareth – even being around him.

She remembered her ambitious daydreams. How flattered she'd been at Gareth's recognition of her abilities and predictions of a rosy future. What a fool she'd been. Welcome to the real world, as Jackie would say.

Retreating from the sordid experience, Yolanda's thoughts returned to Westgate. Her half-formed idea about moving down to the East Kent coast solidified. She wasn't running away from something bad; she was running towards something good. Once again, it seemed an attractive alternative, but she forced herself to consider it rationally. She wasn't so naive as to believe the situation with Gareth could only happen in London, men like him were everywhere. She must set that aside and focus on other issues – facts not feelings.

As usual when faced with a difficult decision, Yolanda made

lists of pros and cons, ranked each, totalled up, compared and analysed.

First, she thought about London. When she'd arrived as a shy young student, that great metropolis loomed over her like an oppressive peak. She fought inch by inch to establish a precarious foothold, no easy climb for the quiet, studious girl. At Nelson Riggs, she'd reached the safety of a plateau, but the only way forward was up, through tricky terrain. Was it worth the effort? No matter how high she climbed, she would still be clinging to that unforgiving rockface. Never able to relax. Always keeping a watchful eye on her fellow mountaineers. Was this really how she wanted to live?

On the other hand, was a small town or village on the Kent coast too much of a backwater? After the initial excitement of the move, would she find working in a provincial law firm uninspiring, even boring? Wasn't it true that she thrived on the pressure, constant challenges and competition at Nelson Riggs?

She would have many more leisure hours; how would she fill them? Down there she only knew a few people, whereas in London she had a wider circle, at least of acquaintances. A crucial factor would be finances, or lack of them. It was easy to talk of reducing expenses, but in practice, how would this work out?

Yolanda tackled all these factors methodically. Surely a job is what you make it? You can find ways to develop in any position.

As to free time, she had discovered new interests, walking, hopefully bike riding, tennis and swimming in the sea in the summer. She could devote more time to art, there was plenty of scope for experimenting and improvement. Cooking was something else to explore.

How many real friends did she have in London, probably only Claudia? She and Joseph could come down to stay. Evenings in the pub would be a comfortable, relaxing end to a day at work, without costing too much. In the end, if the move didn't work out London would still be there.

Suddenly a vision came to her. Herself, sitting in the pub with Robin and the others, she was relaxed and smiling. Yolanda knew immediately what she wanted – a move. She sighed deeply. The overwhelming sense of relief that washed over her, confirmed the decision was the right one. She realised she was ravenous; she'd eaten nothing since the night before. Cheese on toast quickly filled the gap.

Now she'd made the decision to move to the Kent coast, Yolanda identified three things to do. Find a job down there, somewhere to live and rent out her London flat. She started straightaway, sending emails to rental agents and employment agencies.

One of the rental agents called back immediately, and came round in the afternoon. He checked out the flat with a practised eye and named a monthly rental figure she could achieve. Yolanda's face showed her surprise and disappointment.

"I thought it would be higher."

"Lots of one beds available at the moment. Now if you had another bedroom – you'd get a lot more."

But presumably a one-bedroom rental in Westgate would be considerably cheaper.

◆ ◆ ◆

On Sunday, Yolanda had arranged to meet Andy and Claudia at Comic Con. Outside the exhibition centre, the sight of Andy's round face warmed her heart. He greeted her like an old friend and introduced his three mates – self-confessed nerds. Andy hit it off straightaway with Joseph, Claudia's eight-year-old, which would've elicited a sarcastic remark from Robin.

Yolanda wasn't sure what to expect, but found the day surprisingly enjoyable, largely due to Joseph's excitement. The costumes of many of the attendees left him spellbound. Andy and his friends limited themselves to novelty headgear, each wearing a superhero baseball cap, and Joseph immediately asked for one of his own. Claudia frowned.

“Joseph, I said I'd buy you one thing here today. There’ll be lots of other stuff to see – if you get the hat now, you'll be sorry later.”

“They've all got hats. Other people have got costumes. Please Mum, I promise I won't ask for anything else.”

“Would you mind if I bought it for Joseph?” said Yolanda, “Then he'll be one of the gang.”

The boy’s face lit up

“I suppose that's okay. Thanks.”

Andy and his friends found a stall selling the hats and Joseph chose Superman.

“Thanks Yolanda,” he said with a wide smile.

Yolanda and Claudia had trouble keeping up with the boys as they roamed the aisles, calling to each other to point out interesting stalls. They stopped to watch a comic artist at work and Andy quizzed him on his technique.

There were several presentations which were too technical for Yolanda and Claudia, so they found a kids’ corner, where Joseph could decorate a tee shirt. They drank coffee and watched him.

“Andy seems nice,” Claudia said casually.

“Yes.”

“Are you and him – you know, together?”

Yolanda stared at her friend.

“What gave you that idea? No. I like Andy and he's really kind and funny. He's a good artist. But he's just a friend.”

Joseph spent half an hour drawing a picture of Superman and proudly put the tee shirt on.

They all met up for lunch – burgers and chips – and the boys were in heaven.

“Hey Andy, Yolanda says you're a good artist. Are you posting pages from your graphic novel on Instagram? I'd like to see,” Claudia asked him.

“Yes. You can find me at AndyDawsDraws.”

“Great name.”

Joseph listened to Andy and his friends seriously discussing the correct way to apply ketchup to a burger.

“Are you really grown-ups?” he said, “I've never met grown-ups like you before.” Andy’s friends looked sheepish, but he beamed.

“I take that as a great compliment. But Yolanda, promise you won't tell Robin what he said.”

“Who’s Robin?” Claudia asked Yolanda.

“She's our friend down in Westgate. She's always teasing Andy.”

Claudia sighed.

“Oh, I see.”

Yolanda took masses of photos and sent them to Robin.

“The best day ever,” was Joseph's verdict.

◆ ◆ ◆

On Monday morning, Yolanda entered the office with trepidation. She managed to avoid Gareth and he appeared equally reluctant to see her, which was a relief. She worked conscientiously, but for the first time didn’t enjoy the work itself, and found herself watching the clock. She cooked a meal every night, enjoying the food and pleased to save money. It was just a question of forming new habits.

The employment agent set up two phone interviews with law firms in Kent that week, but both quoted a salary range, the highest of which was still a shock to Yolanda.

"With my current position and background, I suppose they'd offer the maximum?"

"I'm afraid not. They always give a range and they always offer the bottom figure."

"Really? But even the top rate's much lower than London."

"That's the reality of life outside London. They'll probably promise to review the salary after six months. That's pretty standard."

This was a shock. She had counted on earning considerably more.

◆ ◆ ◆

On Friday, Yolanda left the office on the dot of five-thirty. Driving along the M25 – even though the traffic was bad – she was relieved to be getting away from London. The lights of the Queen Elizabeth bridge looked even more impressive in the dark, spanning the Thames like a necklace of shimmering pearls. Her heart lifted, as if she was going home.

A light shone over Robin's front door and when she opened it, a welcoming glow spilled out into the dark street. She hugged Yolanda.

"I've missed you."

Yolanda sat at the kitchen table and Robin brought a steaming dish out of the oven.

"I hope you like shepherd's pie?"

"Who doesn't?"

They were still sitting there long after they'd finished eating, catching up on all the news. Yolanda spoke about what had happened with Gareth for the first time, and Robin listened in silence. Then she shook her head.

"I'd have kneed him – where it hurts."

"But he's my boss, I have to work with him."

Robin turned to look at her.

"Do you really? Isn't that harassment – can't you report him? Get him sacked?"

Yolanda had never considered the idea. She was used to relying on herself and living by the laws of the corporate jungle, however unfair. She shrugged.

"It wasn't pleasant, but I've got over it."

Robin went on, "It can't be right that he should get away with it. And he might do it again – to someone who wasn't like you. Who didn't know how to handle him and protect herself."

Yolanda looked at her friend's earnest face. She was right.

"I didn't think of that. It's true, I must do something. I've just got to work out what."

Robin was working on Saturday until the afternoon, and Yolanda was happy to revisit what she thought of as her old haunts – in Westgate and Margate. When Robin got home, she was carrying a large bag.

"I've invited Andy and Pete round tonight. Tash is busy getting ready for the barbecue and Melody's not doing so well at the moment. I brought these back from the shop and we can get fish and chips for a treat."

"I've been wanting to get fish and chips down here – I never got round to it."

The guys turned up with wine, beer and the fish and chips.

"Hi Andy, long time no see," said Yolanda.

"It was great to see you at Comic Con, what did you think of it? I like that kid, what was his name – Joseph? I like kids – I think I'd make a good dad."

"You're just a big kid yourself," said Robin.

"But having a child would make me grow up. Be more

responsible. Hey Robin, what do you think, shall we pair up?"

"That's all I need, be careful, Yolanda, if you spend too much time with Andy you'll turn into a nerd."

"There're worse things," said Yolanda. She smiled at Pete, feeling unaccountably shy.

"Good to have you back," he said.

"Do you really want to move down here?" Andy asked when she told them her plans.

"Yes, but I have to find a job and rent out my flat first."

"By the way," Andy went on, "I tried to look you up on Instagram but I couldn't find you."

"I've never bothered with Instagram."

The others looked shocked.

"I can't believe you're an artist and not on Instagram. It's the most visual social media platform," said Andy, "I post my work all the time – pages from my graphic novel, look." He showed her some images.

"I put up shots of my jewellery, it's a way of marketing, but also, I get ideas and comments from people. I can sell stuff as well." said Pete.

"Shall I set you up with an account?" Andy asked.

"But I've got nothing to put up," said Yolanda.

"Yes, you have," said Robin, "it's not only about finished works of art – you can post sketches, photos, all kinds of things."

She wasn't convinced. While the others were talking, she idly checked 'Georgette' – George's dress shop in Leeds on Instagram. She was amazed to see an up-to-date feed with professional photos of the shop front, displays and George herself looking stunning in some of her garments. Surely Jackie wasn't on Instagram? But no, the account for 'Swish' salons had a similar collection. Those two old birds never missed a trick.

Yolanda asked Andy to set her up with an account. If her mum was on Instagram, she didn't want to be left behind.

CHAPTER 9

"Do you like Pete?"

They were having breakfast when Robin said this, and Yolanda nearly choked on her toast. She prolonged the coughing fit, allowing herself time to prepare a reply.

"He's a nice guy. Kind."

Robin frowned.

"I wasn't sure whether to say anything. It's none of my business. But I don't want you to get hurt."

Yolanda turned to her friend in surprise.

"What do you mean? Is there something I should know about him?"

Robin sighed.

"I don't want to put you off. And he's a nice guy – a good person. Anyway, it probably doesn't mean anything."

Now she was intrigued. Robin went on.

"A couple of years ago, Tash had a friend down to stay for the summer. I can't even remember her name." She stared into the distance. "Gail. It was Gail. She was getting over a bad breakup and wanted to get away. She seemed nice, but quiet and sort of fragile. She hung out with us." Robin smiled. "The Kent coast worked its magic. She opened up, was more cheerful. Pete was very kind to her; you know what he's like. We all were.

"Gail was interested in making jewellery. At least that's what she said." Robin's forehead furrowed. "No, that's unfair. It was probably genuine. Anyway, she asked Pete to show her his work and how he made it. She went over to his house. After that it seemed they were together – an item. She was leaving at the end of the summer, and they were planning for Pete to come and stay with her after, at least she was planning...

"She was already needy, but then she got sort of clingy. Wanted to be with Pete all the time. Expected him to take care of her." Robin shook her head. "It was too much for Pete. We could all see that. Too full on. Too soon. He needs his space and she didn't understand that. Maybe because she was on the rebound...

"Anyway, it came to a head. Something happened and Gail left. In the middle of the night. She went off. She left Tash a note – just a scribble – and we never saw her again. She didn't even get in touch with Tash afterwards.

"Pete went over to France the next day. He stayed away for a couple of weeks and when he came back, we never talked about the whole business.

It probably doesn't mean anything. Gail and Pete weren't suited. I'm sorry, Yolanda, I shouldn't have said any of this."

"No, you were right. I'm glad you did."

As they cleared the table and washed up, Yolanda thought about Robin's words.

We've all had relationships that went wrong. Just look at Mark and me. That type of clingy girl would have suited him. I'm not like that.

It wasn't very nice of Gail to go off. If she'd been staying with Tash all that time... not much of a friend.

Robin's information didn't make any difference to her feelings about Pete.

◆ ◆ ◆

The barbecue was on Sunday. Robin and Yolanda came early to help and found Andy and Pete already there. Tash's home was a garden flat in an old building in Cliftonville. Robin set up the barbecue, Tash and Yolanda made salads, and Pete and Andy moved tables and chairs outside.

Yolanda wasn't sure what sort of guests to expect. There were some from Tash's work at the cathedral, neighbours with children and various others of all ages.

Pete brought her a drink and they sat down at a table.

"I've seen some pieces of your jewellery, what's it made of and how do you make it?"

"It's actually made of acrylic, a kind of plastic. The process is simple, but complicated to describe. Maybe you can come over and I'll show you how I do it. When'll you be down here again?"

"I'm not sure. I'm hoping to have some job interviews. I had a couple on the phone, but I haven't heard back yet."

"It sounds like there're jobs going, then."

"Yes, that's true. I don't want to start looking for a flat down here until the other things are settled. It's all a bit up in the air at the moment."

They were both silent for a while.

"Yolanda..."

She looked at Pete sharply, his tone had changed. He sat up stiffly, hands gripping the arms of his chair.

"Yolanda..."

His shoulders slumped, he bit his lip and looked down. "Never mind." he muttered, "I'll see if the food's ready." He stood up.

She leaned back. What'd just happened? Pete was on the verge of asking her out, she could tell. But he didn't. What made him change his mind?

When he'd gone, A middle-aged woman in a scarlet dress, sat down. She introduced herself as Marion and said she ran the choir that Tash belonged to.

"How do you know Tash?" she asked.

"I live in London and I came down here for a holiday, and met Tash through another friend."

A man in a navy blazer sat down beside Marion.

"This is my husband, Roger Baldwin," she said, "Roger, this is Yolanda, she's a DFL."

"I'm planning to move down here permanently, actually. I'm looking into work and accommodation."

"What line of work are you in?" Roger asked.

"I'm a lawyer, I work for Nelson Riggs."

His eyes widened.

"I see. If you're looking for a job down here, you'll get a shock when you find out about the salaries."

"I know, but the cost of living will be less. And there're other benefits."

"As it so happens," said Roger, "I'm the head of a local law practice, Fletcher and Barnes. We have several offices in the area. Here's my card. Give me a ring if you're really interested."

"Thanks, I will. I suppose you've always lived in the area?"

"I studied in London and worked there for a few years. It didn't suit me, the pressure, watching your back all the time. Don't get me wrong, we work hard at our firm, but we like to think of our staff as part of the family. We're a team. In a place like this, you get to know your clients, I've dealt with several generations in some families and many of them have become friends."

When the rest of the guests had gone, Pete, Yolanda, Robin and Andy stayed to clear up.

"It's been lovely," said Robin hugging Tash.

"I couldn't have done it without your help. And Andy of course."

"He's usually more of a hindrance than a help."

"Oi, I heard that. I don't know what you mean, I've been running around at your beck and call all day."

"You can help me take out the rubbish, to finish the job," she said.

◆ ◆ ◆

Yolanda thought about Robin's suggestion that she should take action against Gareth. She had told Mark she wanted to protect herself. She hadn't given in to Gareth, but she'd been willing to accept his behaviour without doing anything. He had got away scot-free, and was liable to act in the same way again. She was the one feeling uncomfortable, as if she was in the wrong. But what could she do without damaging her career? Eventually she came up with an answer.

On Monday evening, Yolanda paid a satisfactory visit to the Luna bar. The next morning, when she knew he was alone, she went into Gareth's office without knocking and closed the door. Gareth looked startled.

"This isn't the best time, I'm busy right now."

He returned to the computer. Yolanda sat down. She spoke calmly.

"This matter can't wait. Your behaviour to me constitutes sexual harassment and bullying."

His mouth hung open.

"I intend to make a formal complaint to the senior partners, and report the matter to the police."

"Yolanda, you're overreacting. You misunderstood the situation. You had a lot to drink."

As Gareth spoke, his confidence returned. He sat back in his chair, playing with a pen. "You flatter yourself. As I remember, you approached me and asked me to put you forward for promotion. You offered... well let's just say you offered some inducements, which of course I couldn't consider." he smiled. "I can see you're upset, so I'll make allowances for your behaviour, let it go. But you'd better watch your step. I'm sure you won't be so foolish as to say another word on this subject."

He clearly expected her to crawl away with her tail between her legs. Instead, she also sat back in her chair, maintaining an air of quiet confidence. She took out a notebook and opened it.

"That's your story? Interesting. So, you won't mind explaining to the senior partners, your wife and of course the police, why the barman at the Luna bar says you'd been drinking heavily before I arrived, and told him you had a girl from the office lined up for a 'wild night'." She read from the notebook. "You said, 'This one's ambitious – a whiff of promotion and she'll be hooked." She looked at the scarlet-faced man. "The barman said you ordered a soda water, and he saw you add something to the glass, my glass." She closed the notebook.

Gareth dropped his pen; his face was purple.

"I didn't, he couldn't..."

"Since you appear to be lost for words, I'll tell you what's going to happen. I will not report your behaviour to anyone."

He looked relieved.

"On certain conditions. You will sign these two letters I've drafted. The first is an admission of what you've done, and an apology. The second is a reference for me. I do not intend to stay at this firm forever."

She placed two sheets of paper on his desk.

"Read these."

He skimmed the pages and looked up.

"Now sign them."

he hesitated, as if ready to protest, but after a look at Yolanda's implacable expression, he signed his name twice. She leant over, picked up the letters and walked out of the room. Her heart was pounding with relief and triumph, but her face showed nothing.

The next day Jackie rang.

"What's happening about the promotion?" she said without preamble, "Is it definite yet?"

Yolanda sighed.

"The promotion's not going to happen, Mum."

"Why not? What did you do? How did you manage to mess it up?"

Yolanda wanted to silence her mum, shock her.

"There were strings attached I couldn't stomach. My boss wanted me to sleep with him."

Jackie said nothing at first.

"How much are we talking about? How much of a pay rise?"

"What difference does that make, Mum?"

"Yolanda don't be so naive. You're not a child. Sometimes you get an opportunity. If you handle it right... I'd have done anything to break into the American market."

Yolanda couldn't take in what she was hearing. She ended the call.

◆ ◆ ◆

A short while later, the phone rang again. Surely Jackie wasn't ringing to apologise. But this call wasn't from Jackie. It was the employment agent, to say the firms that had interviewed Yolanda wanted to meet her in person. They arranged for her to go down on the Thursday and see both of them. As she'd have finished by early afternoon, Yolanda rang Roger Baldwin and set up a meeting afterwards with him.

◆ ◆ ◆

At the art class on Wednesday evening, the teacher was pleased with Yolanda's work.

"You're going in the right direction; it'll look great at the exhibition. Are you posting?"

"Posting… you mean?"

"Instagram. People like to see progress; it generates interest for you and the show."

"Are you on Instagram?" Yolanda asked Claudia. She looked puzzled.

"Have you still not got an account?"

"I've just got an account, but I haven't put up anything yet. Andy showed me what to do, but..."

"How is Andy, Joseph is still talking about him? I'll show you how to post, if you want to try now."

Yolanda was relieved to find the process so straightforward.

"I post at least once a week," said Claudia, "and I've already got a few followers."

Yolanda decided even though she didn't officially have any leave left, she'd take time off work to attend interviews. Gareth was unlikely to complain – and anyway she had his glowing reference. She sent a vague email saying she'd be out of the office and took the train down to Margate the next morning. She opened Instagram on her phone and looked at Robin's account. She saw Tash and Andy had commented on Robin's latest painting. Then she went on to Andy and Pete. She scrolled back through images of Pete's delicate pieces of jewellery. He had a lot of followers. Then, almost as an afterthought, she looked at her own account. She was amazed that the images she'd uploaded the previous evening, had already received comments. They were both from Pete, with praise and encouragement. Her heart glowed. How kind of him. Now she understood the appeal of Instagram.

◆ ◆ ◆

Yolanda's first appointment was in Ramsgate, the next town along the coast after Broadstairs. The small firm had only been established for two years, and Simon Oakridge, the owner, interviewed her himself. Simon was younger than she expected. His suit and the office decor were surprisingly similar to that of her own firm in London, though on a smaller scale. Simon exuded confidence and drive. Nelson Riggs, her current employer, clearly impressed him. He took it for granted she'd wish to continue her career in the same kind of dynamic (his word) environment. His questions weren't challenging and she was well prepared. He seemed to be keener to describe his vision than find out about her.

"Yolanda, I can see you have ambition, you're a go getter. That's just the sort of person we want. Someone who takes no prisoners, gives their all. Makes things happen. My vision is a new breed of lawyers. We may not be located in a big city, but we aim to function like a big city firm.

"I started my career at Fletcher and Barnes. Now don't get me wrong, Roger Baldwin's a lovely guy, straight as they come, but old fashioned. He has no idea how to hustle. It's all very well to be a gentlemen, play fair and so on – one big happy family – but that doesn't cut it nowadays. In this business you have to take risks, go the extra mile.

"I can't offer you a huge salary to start with, but we operate on a bonus scheme. You do well, win cases, bring in clients and I can promise you won't lose out."

He sat back, looking into the distance, his eyes glowing as if caught up in his own eloquence.

She had heard enough.

◆ ◆ ◆

The second interview didn't get off to a good start. The woman who interviewed her – one of the partners – reminded her of Jackie, and not in a good way. It wasn't so much what the woman said, but her manner, which was humourless and intense. Yolanda recognised this was her own prejudice, but relevant nonetheless and not to be ignored.

In contrast, Roger Baldwin was genial and relaxed. He seemed genuinely pleased to see Yolanda again. The hour's conversation, on the surface, wasn't a grilling, but she noticed the subtle, searching questions he included. She'd researched his company and already knew it had a good reputation and was large, with offices in Margate, Broadstairs, Ramsgate and Canterbury, this was her chance to get a feel for the operation, and how she could fit in.

Yolanda boarded the train back to London exhausted. Fortified by a latte and a sandwich, she reviewed the three interviews while they were fresh in her mind. The first one she immediately discounted. Simon Oakridge and his 'vision' was exactly what she was trying to get away from. The woman at the second firm – perhaps for irrational reasons – made her frown. Not a good start. This job was also rejected.

That left Roger Baldwin. This was the best option. She liked the man personally, and the firm was well established, with a good reputation. In addition, it was large enough to offer scope for development. This was all very well, but it would be better to wait and see if Roger made an offer before getting excited. She sat back and closed her eyes.

◆ ◆ ◆

On Friday morning, the employment agent called to let Yolanda know both of the law firms had offered her jobs. She stalled the agent, waiting to hear from Roger Baldwin and was relieved when he rang her personally, later in the day. He said he was delighted to offer her a position at his Ramsgate office. The salary he mentioned was what she was expecting, in line with one of the other offers. The salary Simon Oakridge proposed was lower, but no doubt he thought the mention of bonuses and other vague inducements would make up for this. Yolanda accepted Roger's offer on the spot and they set a date in six weeks' time for her to start. She sat back and let her breath out. To her relief – and Gareth's – Yolanda handed in her notice. The first step to her new life was accomplished.

◆ ◆ ◆

Now she'd secured a suitable job, she chased up the rental agent handling her flat. He'd shown it to a number of potential renters, who expressed interest, but needed her to give him a definite date before taking the matter further. She'd hoped to get a higher rent than he predicted, but this wasn't to be. In the end a pleasant young couple agreed a reasonable figure and wanted to move in within a month. The initial contract was to be for six months, with the option to extend. The agent was bringing them round the following evening to sign the paperwork. This was a big relief. The numbers were working out. Everything would be alright.

However, her relief was premature, the agent called the next morning to say the renters couldn't sign until the following week, but assured her they were still keen and suggested she give them a deadline.

With this in hand, Yolanda focused on her Westgate accommodation. After searching online, she spoke to a selection of estate agents on the phone. She discovered the type of rental she wanted was limited in the Westgate area, was she willing to look further afield? Moving inland, further from the sea would be cheaper, but she baulked at this. What was the point of moving down there if she had to drive to the beach? The agent suggested Ramsgate, where she'd be working, but she didn't know the area. Public transport was also important, she preferred to be able to walk to a station. Margate was busier and noisier than Westgate, but cheaper. Overwhelmed by all the conflicting criteria, in the end, Yolanda told a couple of agents her requirements and let them select suitable flats and set up viewings for the following weekend.

Robin said Yolanda was welcome to stay with her and could look at flats on Sunday, but was working on the Saturday. She must've told Andy, because he immediately called Yolanda to say he'd go round with her on the Saturday. She was touched.

Andy picked her up and they looked at a couple of properties nearby. Andy meant well, but his priorities and interests didn't correspond with Yolanda's. He discounted one place because there was no wall for his oversized TV screen, and overlooked a minuscule kitchen in the other, because the only cooking he did was to heat up pizzas. However, he did remind her of the importance of dedicated parking. With an hour until the next appointment, they headed into Margate Old Town for coffee. As they passed the Turner Centre, Andy went to the shop and Yolanda checked out the information in the lobby about forthcoming exhibitions.

"Hello Yolanda," she turned at the familiar voice. There was Pete, carrying a cardboard box.

"I heard you were down; I'm doing my deliveries."

She smiled at him.

"Nice to see you."

"I won't be long, maybe we can grab a coffee," Pete said.

Andy came back.

"Hi Pete. Sorry to keep you waiting, Yolanda, they didn't have what I wanted. We'd better get going."

Pete looked surprised.

"I'm viewing flats to rent," said Yolanda.

Pete stared after them.

At the end of the day there was one flat Yolanda preferred to the others and it was in Westgate. But she had more to see the next day.

That evening Tash invited Robin and Yolanda to her home, and Yolanda wasn't surprised when Pete and Andy arrived. However, for once, Pete didn't look at her and barely acknowledged her friendly greeting. He was clearly in a bad mood and unfortunately the food hadn't turned out well, so Tash was upset and kept apologising.

Andy said, "I'm used to burnt pizza," and other unhelpful comments until Robin told him to shut up.

"How's Melody?" asked Yolanda, "I haven't seen her for a while."

Robin sighed.

"It's difficult – it's a shame. She hasn't been doing well. She needs looking after, so she's gone to stay with her parents."

"I'm sorry, but she's lucky to have parents like that." She tried to imagine Jackie's reaction in similar circumstances.

"My mum and dad are cool," said Andy, "they're coming down in the summer. They love the beach and I get some good home cooking."

Robin glared at him.

Yolanda couldn't understand what was the matter with Pete. He seemed to be annoyed with her. When Andy showed Tash and Robin photos of the flats they'd seen, Pete left the table and sat down on the sofa. Not sure if it was the right thing to do, Yolanda sat beside him.

"Thanks for all the nice things you've been posting on my Instagram, I'm really getting into it."

Pete didn't smile, but his expression relaxed.

"I can't wait to move down here," she said, "I feel like a yoyo going backwards and forwards to London. Although Robin's so kind to let me stay all the time."

She smiled and Pete turned his face towards her, but just then Andy called.

"Yolanda, come and tell Robin I really helped you looking at the flats – she doesn't believe it."

Pete scowled and looked down at his phone. A few minutes later he got up and left, with barely a nod at Yolanda. She wondered why he was in such a bad mood. She'd heard him mention problems before – of course everyone had problems – but he seemed to have changed his attitude towards her. She was sure he liked her, but if his interest wore off so quickly, it couldn't have been very strong.

Then she thought of something. The change started that morning at the Turner Centre, when she bumped into Pete. He asked her to go for coffee and then Andy turned up. Pete was surprised to see him. Did he think she liked Andy, that were they going out together? It made sense. How would Pete know they were just looking at flats? He could've asked, but he was sensitive, reserved. He wouldn't push himself forward. If he thought she liked Andy, he'd retreat. That must be the reason. But what to do about it? Yolanda liked Pete and she didn't want to drive him away because of a misunderstanding.

◆ ◆ ◆

On Sunday, she viewed more flats with Robin. She decided the one she'd seen the day before, the one in Westgate was the most suitable. It was a one-bedroom conversion on the first floor of an old house in a quaint square, close to the shops and station. It was smaller than she really wanted, but was willing to compromise for the location. She was reluctant to sign for the flat before the potential tenants had committed to her property in London, but the agent warned her there were other interested parties. Though Yolanda would've advised her clients not to do so in similar circumstances, by the time she left on Sunday evening she'd signed the contract.

Driving back to London, Yolanda thought of Jackie. She'd have to speak to her. Tell her about the move. Maybe it would be better face to face? She didn't relish the prospect, but it had to be done.

CHAPTER 10

The following Saturday morning Yolanda found herself on the train speeding towards Leeds. The house where Jackie currently lived, wasn't the one Yolanda grew up in. That was a small flat. Over the years, as soon as she could, Jackie bought larger and larger properties. She moved into this substantial, detached house, when Yolanda went off to university. Jackie had good taste, an eye for design and quality, but no gift for making a house a home. Each house she occupied was kept in pristine condition, impeccably clean and tidy at all times. Every carefully chosen item had its place, and none was chosen with a child in mind. Growing up, Yolanda felt inhibited by her home. Not an untidy or boisterous child, she could feel Jackie's eyes on her if she so much as made a dent in a cushion. She tried to be as still as possible, and to take up as little space. Only in her own bedroom could she breathe freely and release her elbows from her sides.

The worst example of Jackie's attitude, happened when Yolanda, aged ten, fell over on the way home from school and badly gashed her knee. She limped home, crying and bleeding. When Jackie opened the door, she yelled at the miserable girl.

"Wait! Don't come in," she cried in an agonised tone. She ran to fetch an old towel and threw this at Yolanda, with the peremptory command. "Clean yourself up."

She wouldn't let the sobbing girl inside the house until she'd done so.

Jackie liked to have orchids around the place. But to Yolanda, these weren't friendly, forgiving flowers like roses or lilies. Flowers that were part of the family. Orchids were elegant and aloof like exotic houseguests.

Yolanda thought of George's house. Much as George would've liked her home to mirror her friend's, she couldn't control Tony. Jolly, messy, clumsy Tony like to 'spread himself' and if unchecked would leave his possessions everywhere. The pair came to a compromise and he took over the kitchen and adjoining small snug – the only cosy rooms in the house. Yolanda spent as much time there as she could.

She'd rung to say she was coming, but Jackie's replies were curt, and she was unsure of her welcome. Taking a deep breath, she marched up to the front door, feeling as if she was approaching a battlefield. Jackie opened the door, looking immaculate as usual in leather trousers and cashmere sweater.

"What's the matter with your hair? It looks terrible, I'll ring the salon and ask them to fit you in."

This was Jackie's greeting, delivered before Yolanda had set foot inside the house.

"I hope you've got something good to tell me," Jackie went on with a stony expression.

I'm fine, thanks for asking. Yolanda couldn't help thinking.

"I don't know whether you'll think it's good, but I'm pleased." Yolanda saw she was to get no encouragement and went on. "I'm moving down to the Kent coast – Westgate-on-Sea. I've got a job there."

There was a prolonged silence, during which Yolanda's heart hammered on her ribs. Finally, Jackie looked at her.

"What do you expect me to say? What possible reason could you have for doing this? Is there something I'm missing?"

"If you want to know why, I'll try and explain. I'm not happy working in my current job, I haven't been happy there for a long time – the atmosphere is toxic. I find London life too noisy and hectic. I don't have any real friends there. I went to Westgate on holiday and realised I could live a much better life down there. Better for me.

"The area's beautiful, and the people are different. I've already made a group of friends. I'll be working in an old established firm with a good reputation, in a much more pleasant environment. The cost of living is less, and I'll be living in a different way down there."

Jackie let her speak without interruption and then turned a cool gaze on her daughter.

"It sounds like paradise," she said with a sneer, "but you're forgetting one thing – real life's not like that."

She shook her head.

"I thought you'd have learned more from me. None of these wonderful things you talk about matter. In the end, you can only count on yourself, and what matters is money in the bank.

"You've had it too easy, never gone without, had everything you want. You have no idea how hard it is when you have nothing. I've never told you the whole story – about what happened to me... I think it's time."

Yolanda stiffened. What was she about to hear?

"A couple of years after college I got a job in London. It was the early eighties and the top hairdressers were celebrities. John Frieda, Nicky Clarke, Daniel Galvin," she murmured, "rich and famous people came in all the time. If I'd stayed on in London... The opportunities... I could've made my name. I'd be in America now instead of stuck here."

Jackie stared into the distance and said nothing for a while.

"Marco was the senior stylist... A couple of the girls warned me not to get involved, but I thought they were jealous. He said he was going to open his own salon; we'd get married."

Jackie snorted.

"I believed every word. Until I found I was pregnant – and Marco was already married. I had no choice. I had to go home to Leeds. With nothing. I started again at the bottom. It was hard, but I worked my way up until I was managing a salon. After years of slog, I had the chance to buy out the owner. I got a loan. It was a huge risk, and then I was afraid the business would fail... But I made good, went from strength to strength."

Jackie sat back and sighed as if with relief.

"From everything that happened, I learned I had to stand on my own feet. Not to trust anyone. I wanted you to have the best and make the most of it. If you take life seriously from a young age, you've got a head start.

"You say you want a 'good' life by the seaside. Try living on a low income and you'll see how good that feels. And meanwhile, you'll have lost your place on the ladder. And what're you going to do with the flat?"

"I'm going to rent it out and rent something in Kent, property's cheaper down there."

"Don't forget whose money is in that flat. I paid the deposit. You wouldn't have it without me."

"You know I've always been grateful, Mum. I really appreciate your help."

"Not so grateful that you took my advice even then. I told you to get a two bedroom so you could rent one out to help with the mortgage. I still can't understand why you didn't."

Yolanda sighed; they'd been over this point many times. Her mum hated the idea of paying rent, and owned all the buildings that housed her salons, and a portfolio of other commercial properties. She pushed Yolanda to buy a flat as soon as she had a job in London. She offered to pay the deposit, but when Yolanda realised there were strings attached to the gift, she refused.

Jackie wanted to tell her what flat to buy and where. After university and law school, she was fed up with communal living and longed for her own space. In the end, Jackie's strength of feeling against her daughter 'lining the pockets of landlords', overcame her desire to control her. This was the only time Yolanda remembered standing up to her mum and getting her own way.

"Mum, I want different things from you. Enough to live on – of course I don't want to be poor – but my wants are simpler. I don't need a big house. I want to work in a nice environment without backstabbing. I want to be able to walk on the beach, spend time with friends – real, good friends who help each other."

Jackie scowled.

"I suppose among these 'good friends', there's a man?" she said.

Yolanda was caught off guard.

"Well, yes, maybe – I'm not sure."

"And what does he do, your friend?"

"He's got a jewellery business."

Jackie looked surprised.

"Jewellery, really? What kind of operation – retail, wholesale?"

"He designs and makes the jewellery and distributes it to suppliers around the country and abroad."

"Have you seen the books? What level of business is he doing?"

"No, I haven't –"

Jackie interrupted.

"How many employees?"

"It's just him..."

Now she frowned.

"Just him? What kind of products? Does he specialise – one off pieces or general? Gold, diamonds?"

Yolanda couldn't lie.

"None of those. His jewellery's made of acrylic."

"What do you mean acrylic, what's that?"

Yolanda looked down, her voice shaking.

"It's a kind of plastic."

"Plastic?" Jackie shook her head. "You poor fool. He's heard where you come from – he's found out about me. How much I'm worth. He thinks he's going to get his hands on my money."

Yolanda burst out,

"So, you think no man could love me for myself – the only reason someone would be with me is for my money. Sorry, I mean your money."

Jackie ignored her.

"This man of yours – he sounds like Tony."

"Tony?"

"You know, George's husband. He's a waste of space. No ambition, drive. He lives on George's money."

"But he had a job, wasn't he a carpenter?"

"Carpenter – huh – what sort of job's that? Though he could've made something of it. No, he's just held her back. Without him, she could've done great things."

"But the shop, I thought it was doing so well..."

"It is, that's the point. She could open up more branches around the country. There's no limit. But Tony's always on at her not to work so hard, spend time with him. I don't know why she didn't ditch him years ago.

"He wants to go up to London with her on her buying trips. She won't have it. He'd cramp her style. And he wanted to see you. I soon stopped that idea."

"Why Mum? I didn't know – you didn't tell me. I'd love to see Tony."

Jackie took no notice.

"And another thing – my will. As it stands now, you'll inherit all my money – this house, the salons, the other properties. I'm not having everything I've worked for squandered by someone who sells plastic jewellery." The last words were delivered with contempt. "The way you're carrying on – throwing away a good career for some romantic dream of love by the sea, you're not fit to deal with assets like that. Unless you pull yourself together and see sense, I'm going to change my will. I'll leave everything to George, she's the only one with any brains."

"I don't care about your money. I don't want your money. Can't you understand? I've got enough. I never think about your money – it means nothing to me."

Jackie gave a mirthless laugh.

"Oh really. I bet your friend won't agree. As soon as he finds out you're not getting anything, he'll be off. Stop being so blind. Money protects you. People let you down, take advantage of you."

They'd reached an impasse. Neither of them spoke for a while. Finally, Jackie tried again.

"I understand you're not like me. You want to find a partner. That's not the problem. If it was someone suitable. Another lawyer, someone you met at the office. Doing as well as you, or better. Who had ambition and wanted to get on in the world. Haven't you met any nice lawyers?"

"There was somebody," she spoke reluctantly, as if the words were dragged out of her. "We were together for a while..."

"That's what I mean. I wouldn't mind someone like that."

Yolanda said nothing. So now Mark would be suitable. She hadn't dared tell Jackie about him at the time. But now... he was better than Pete.

Jackie took her silence as a sign she was weakening, having doubts about Pete and pursued her advantage.

"Under those circumstances – if you got back with him, or someone like that..."

"Mum, I wasn't happy with him. Don't you want me to be happy?" Yolanda looked at her mother. "Mum, do you love me?"

"What?"

"Do you love me? It's a simple enough question."

"Haven't I always looked after you? Done everything for you? Given you the best school, clothes. I've worked my whole life for you. To give you security – a future. Isn't that – love?"

She had trouble even saying the word.

"If you really love someone, you let them live their own life, even if you don't agree. Allow them to make their own choices."

"But what you're doing is wrong... a mistake."

"Mum, I truly appreciate everything you've done for me. I know you always did what you thought was best. But now, now is the time for me to live the way I want."

Jackie said nothing and Yolanda sat still, unconsciously holding her breath. Jackie stroked the arm of her Italian designer sofa with perfectly manicured fingers. For a moment, the long, blood red nails looked like talons, clawing at the fabric. Yolanda shuddered.

Jackie looked up.

"I can't let you throw away everything I've worked for. If you do this – I've got no choice. I'm going to change my will. But if you come to your senses, give up this crazy idea..."

Yolanda let her breath out in a sigh. It was no use. She left the house.

Jackie's words had given her an idea. She walked down the road in the opposite direction to the station, turned the corner and a few minutes later, knocked on the front door of another impressive, opulent house. It was opened by a bald man in his sixties with a cheerful expression. His face registered amazement.

"Why it's Yolanda, I haven't seen you for ages. How're you, lass?"

She couldn't speak. She was exhausted. Drained. The sight of his well-loved, concerned face after Jackie's hardness was too much.

"Tony…" Tears trickled down her cheeks.

"Now, now, let's have none of that. Come inside. What's going on? Who's been upsetting you? Though I suppose I can guess. Let's hear it all, what does she say you've done wrong?"

Yolanda told him everything, about her life in London, the plans to go to Westgate, Pete. She didn't mention Jackie's remarks about Tony himself. He shook his head from time to time and tutted.

"She's a hard woman, is Jackie. Life's given her some tough breaks, but no more than plenty of other folk. And she's done so well in business – like George. She could've slowed down years ago. But it was never enough – she always wanted more. More salons more money. America…

"Even when you were little, she worked too hard. I used to think, *she won't be young for long, spend time with her.* Do you remember you and me – we had fun together?" he smiled at the memory.

"Of course, Tony. I used to pretend – it was a kind of game – that you were my dad."

His eyes widened.

"I wished you were my little girl, my daughter."

"You and George never had kids."

He sighed.

"No, we got married young and George wanted to start her business. Then the business began to take off and it wasn't the right time. It was never the right time. But I had you."

She took his hands.

"It's so nice to see you again."

"I've said to George I wanted to come up to London with her. We could stay in a hotel, make a holiday of it. I said we could see you – but she never wanted to. No time. You know what she's like. And your mum, I don't think she wanted us to get together. Whenever I asked for your phone number, there was always an excuse. I thought you didn't want to see me."

"No, that's not true. I never thought you were interested. I thought you were just being kind to me when I was a kid. I didn't realise – otherwise of course I'd have been in touch. I'd have loved to meet up with you in London.

"But now I'm going to be living by the sea it's even better. Tony, it's such a beautiful place, the beaches, everything. And you can meet my friends, you'd like them – they're like us. Not like my mum..."

"Would you really want me to come?"

"Yes, I've got a sofa bed, you'll always be welcome."

"Yolanda," Tony looked serious, "I'm so proud of you. How you've turned out."

He hugged her.

"Now lass, are you hungry? I know you won't have been offered a bite to eat in that house."

She realised she was starving.

"George is away in Italy; we can do what we like."

He fed her egg and chips and it was like old times. In the end she stayed over with Tony and he took her to the station the next day. He hugged her.

"Maybe I'm wrong, maybe I'm speaking out of turn. She is your mum, but..." Tony hesitated as if unsure whether or not to go on. "No, I must warn you. Jackie can be a dangerous enemy. I've seen some things..." he shook his head. "I know you're her daughter, but she can't stand being crossed – even by you." he looked into her eyes. "Be careful, lass."

"Thanks for everything, keep in touch," she said.

"Don't worry, now that I've found you again, you won't get rid of me so easily."

◆ ◆ ◆

Sitting on the train, Yolanda could still feel Tony's bear hug. She smiled. Good old Tony. How could she have thought he didn't really care about her? If she hadn't decided to go and look him up... She frowned. It was Jackie again, mixing in, controlling her life, deciding who she could see.

Leaning back in her seat, Yolanda relaxed until the ring of her phone awoke her from a doze. It was Robin.

"How's it going? How's it working out with your mum?"

"I'm glad I came and I've sorted some stuff out. How're things with you?"

"I'm fine. I'm ringing because I just had a strange conversation with Pete."

"Pete?" Yolanda sat up.

"Yes. He just rang and asked me if you're involved with Andy – seeing him."

"What did you tell him?"

"The truth. I said I was sure you're not. Where could he have got that idea?"

"I think I know, when I was looking at flats with Andy, we went into Margate for a coffee and Pete saw us together."

"It still sounds strange to me. You don't like Andy, do you?"

"I like Andy very much as a friend – he's a lovely guy. But not in that way."

"Oh, I see." Did she detect relief in Robin's voice? That was also strange. But at least now Pete knew he had no reason to be jealous. How complicated life could be.

◆ ◆ ◆

Yolanda's flat was still not rented out. The couple who were initially interested, missed the deadline, and continued to make excuses for not signing until the agent agreed they weren't serious. Unfortunately, a flood of one-bedroom flats in the area had just come onto the market, and renters who'd previously shown interest in her flat had found alternatives. The agent was always hopeful, but in the end, he suggested reducing the price. Finally, after a lengthy phone negotiation, Yolanda came to an agreement with a young executive, and they arranged to meet at the agent's office the following evening to sign the contract.

However, this wasn't to be. The next morning, Yolanda received a letter from the Freeholder of her flat, Headstart Property Holdings. As with most flats in England, Yolanda was only a leaseholder, albeit with a 120-year lease. The Freeholder owned the building. She'd had little to do with the Freeholder since she'd bought the flat and had so far encountered no difficulties. This letter changed everything. She read, with horror.

HEADSTART PROPERTY HOLDINGS

Re: 12 Hillcrest Rd, West Hampstead

To the Leaseholders of flats: 1, 2, 3, 4, 5, 6

The Freeholder will be carrying out extensive work to the property, consisting of essential repairs and improvements. The work will be both internal and external.

The Freeholder, their Agent and Contractors will require access to the flats, both for inspection and to carry out the work, as stated in the lease. Leaseholders will be contacted shortly to arrange the initial visits.

The external work will involve the erection of scaffolding at both the front and rear of the property.

It is estimated that all work will be completed within six months, if no unforeseen issues arise.

The Freeholder regrets any inconvenience to the Leaseholders, but the final result should prove beneficial to all.

The timing couldn't be worse. Yolanda was legally and morally bound to inform the prospective renter of this development, which would involve a considerable amount of inconvenience and noise. No tenant in their right mind would sign a rental agreement under the circumstances. Her flat was unrentable, at least for six months and maybe more.

Recovering from her initial shock, she scrutinised the letter. Who were Headstart Property Holdings? A quick check online gave her the answer. The name of the director of Headstart Property Holdings was the same as that of Swish Salons Ltd. Jackie Blake. Yolanda's mum.

Now it all made sense. The timing of the project ensuring a six-month disruption to the building was no coincidence. Further investigation revealed Jackie had bought the Freehold of 12 Hillcrest Rd at the same time as Yolanda bought her flat in the building. She'd never told her daughter. Now Jackie was using the Freehold as a weapon. A way of forcing Yolanda to give up her plan to move to Westgate, by removing the rental income from her flat. The income she was relying on.

She marvelled at her mum's actions. Was Jackie's motive truly that of concern? Or was it a desire to show she was right and Yolanda was wrong? Did she care about Yolanda's welfare or was she willing to sacrifice her daughter's happiness to prove a point? Yolanda didn't know, but Jackie's behaviour alarmed her. She remembered Tony's words of warning. Unwillingly, she faced the question. Would Jackie destroy her own daughter in her obsession for control?

A cold hand gripped Yolanda's heart. She felt sick. She was committed to the move. Committed to paying rent on the flat in Westgate. On a reduced salary. How could she manage?

She sat still while ideas raced through her mind, but gradually the panic lessened. Her sensible, logical brain reasserted itself. She wouldn't be destitute. Other people lived on far less. There must be a way.

She had two options. Earn more or spend less. Could she earn more? Take on another job? But even if she could find work in the evenings or weekends, would that be wise? She'd have enough on her plate, relocating and starting a new job. That wasn't a sensible option. At least at first, until she'd settled down.

Could she get money another way? There were her savings – a not insubstantial amount – but she baulked at this. All the years with Jackie had reinforced the conviction that savings were her security. She'd only use them as the last resort, if every other avenue failed.

That left only one choice. Spend less. Jackie had challenged her to live on a lower income and now it was time to step up to that challenge. Yolanda frowned. Hadn't she heard of a website that helped people save money on everyday expenses? Somebody mentioned it in the pub. Frugal Life..., was it called? Google quickly threw up 'Frugal Living' and she dived in.

She spent all her spare time over the next few days researching the topic. 'Frugal Living' was more than a website advising on how to save money. It was a way of life, akin to a religious movement. Delving deep into the rabbit hole on the internet, she followed links to other related sites as well as Facebook groups, devouring everything she came across. It was fascinating.

Yolanda had always kept a check on her finances, never going into debt and saving regularly from her first job in the hair salon. But this new information was a revelation. 'Frugal Living' showed ways of saving on almost every aspect of her life. Admittedly each one wasn't a huge sum in itself, but the total effect was substantial, significant.

She completed a questionnaire which forced her to question everything she'd regarded as a necessity. A few of these she was able to downgrade to luxuries and discovered cheaper alternatives to many others. However, whichever way Yolanda looked at the numbers, they didn't add up. As well as her living expenses in Westgate, there'd be ongoing costs for her flat in London – even if it stood empty. Waves of panic overwhelmed her. She went through the figures again and again. Even with her salary in Westgate, and reducing her expenditure to the bone, there was a shortfall. For now, a part time job wasn't the answer. Where was the money to come from?

When she calmed down, Yolanda thought about her savings. Jackie had trained her to save as much as possible, for the future and to maintain an emergency fund. Jackie drummed into her, 'An emergency fund is only for real emergencies'. Unexpected expenses that couldn't be avoided. Nothing else. But Yolanda had made the choice to commit herself to renting the flat in Westgate without waiting for confirmation of her London rental income. She'd made a mistake. But was it an emergency?

She remembered something else. Her mum was equally vehement on the subject of loans. Or at least she had been, adapting the adage to, 'Never a borrower be.' However, telling the story of her past, the early days of her business, she admitted she'd taken out a loan – a big risk at the time – to buy her first salon.

If Yolanda was in control of her own life, she could decide what was an emergency and how to use her savings. If she wanted to give her new life in Westgate the best chance of success – using her savings to supplement her income for a few months – or even longer, was an investment. She could afford the money; her mindset was the problem.

She decided this was the best option. The sums involved were small. However, at times a feeling of dread came over her, at what she was doing. This was the reality of living on a lower income. This anxiety clutching at the heart, the feelings of panic. Perhaps Jackie was really trying to teach her a lesson. Was this her way of showing love?

◆ ◆ ◆

The next day, in the early evening Yolanda's doorbell rang. A motorbike courier handed her a large brown envelope and a clipboard. Mechanically she signed her name, wondering what it could be. She opened the envelope, and took out a sheet of paper.

Holmes Investigation Agency

Confidential background report

Subject: Pete Venables

Home address: Swallow Cottage, Lime Lane, Thanet, Kent

Business Address: As above

Age: 33

As requested, time being of the essence, this is an interim report based on an expedited initial investigation.

The Subject is currently the owner and sole proprietor of a jewellery business trading under the name 'Madi'. The business was established in 19- - by Madeleine Venables.

The Subject began working for Ms Venables in 20- -, when he moved into her residence. At that time, the subject was 23 years old and Ms Venables, 59. The exact nature of their relationship is not known.

In 20- -, Ms Venables made a will leaving her business, property (Swallow Cottage) and all other assets to the Subject. She had no relations. Nine months later, Ms Venables died suddenly. The Subject continues to reside at the above address and continues as sole proprietor of the jewellery business. Total assets unknown.

At this stage it has been impossible to establish any information about the Subject prior to 20- -. No employment history or family background could be found.

If required, a more thorough search could be conducted.

◆ ◆ ◆

Yolanda stared at the report in bewilderment. Someone had commissioned a private investigator to look into Pete's background. But who? Why? And why'd they sent it to her?

It had to be Jackie. Another attempt to interfere with her plans. She wanted to discredit Pete – put Yolanda wise to the truth about him – she'd claim. She shook her head. Were there any lengths to which her mum wouldn't go?

She read the report again. Seeing the facts on paper – although they were known to her – made Yolanda uncomfortable. As a lawyer, she was used to such documents, but this was different. She had feelings for Pete. Even though she'd no hand in commissioning the report, She had caused this intrusion into Pete's private life. Jackie had done this because of her. If Pete found out... Yolanda was appalled at the idea. Against all her legal training, she nearly tore up the report and threw it away.

But slowly, insidiously, doubts crept in. As they were reported, the facts had an unsavoury slant. How well did she really know Pete? He'd given her his version of events. Maybe there was another one. Although she tried to ignore it, one sentence stuck out. '*The exact nature of their relationship is not known.*' The wording was unpleasant and suggestive. The implication Madi's money had inspired Pete's interest in her, was clear. The circumstances of her death could be regarded as sinister... But this was all nonsense, Pete had told her about Madi.

If only Pete was there, in front of her, she'd know. She'd ask him...

But of course, she would do no such thing. She felt hot and cold at the idea. He must never find out about the report.

This time Jackie's arrow had hit the mark.

There were a great many more loose ends to tie up than Yolanda expected. The smallest tasks caused the most trouble. Although she'd hardly used the gym since she broke up with Mark, she was still paying for it. Despite emails and phone calls, cancelling her membership proved difficult. In the end, she went there in person.

"Hey Yolanda!"

It was Mark, looking taller and fitter than ever, his hair thicker and eyes bluer. She'd forgotten how handsome he was.

"I haven't seen you here for ages, I didn't think you were still a member."

She couldn't help returning his smile.

"Have you got time for a drink?"

Why not? What'd she got to lose? But no green sludge. She ordered the sweetest, most unhealthy coffee and watched Mark's face. He didn't react.

"It's so good to see you. You look tanned, have you been away?"

"Yes, I have actually."

He'd never guess where. Westgate wasn't on Mark's radar.

"How's work?" she asked.

"Same old rat race."

Yolanda was surprised at his tone. She'd never heard him anything but enthusiastic about his job.

"Are you still with Nelson Riggs?"

"No, I'm starting a new job soon."

"Oh, where?"

It would be churlish to prevaricate.

"I'm moving out of London, to a small town."

Once again, Mark's response was unexpected.

"You're not the only one. A few people I know have moved to the country. An old pal of mine – bumped into him the other day – he's moved to the coast. Property is much cheaper; he's got a house with a sea view. He was telling me he has a better work life balance. Where exactly will you be living?"

"The Kent coast," she admitted.

Mark frowned.

"Somewhere near Canterbury?"

"That's right."

"It's not a place called – what was it? Whitstable?"

Even more surprising.

"In the general area."

"What a coincidence. My pal lives in Whitstable. Couldn't stop raving about it."

Mark looked into her eyes.

"I've missed you so much. You're not like other girls. I realise that now. You need your own space. I wish..." he looked down. "I've changed, I really have. I didn't understand you, appreciate you. I thought about getting in touch so many times, but now it's happened... Will you give me another chance? Let me prove to you I've changed?"

"I'm moving, Mark..."

"I know, but I could come down and visit – for a weekend. Take things slowly. My pal said I can come any time I want. What do you think?"

He took hold of her hand, but stopped himself quickly, and let it go. The citrus tang of his aftershave brought back memories.

Had he really changed? Maybe it was worth another chance?

What harm could it do if he visited her? There was nothing really between her and Pete. That unsettling report was fresh in her mind. It would solve the problem with Jackie, a little voice murmured in her ear. No more trouble there... Mark had a lot of good qualities. If he'd really changed...

"I don't know," she said slowly.

Encouraged by her indecision, he went on.

"Did you say you've got a job down there?"

"Yes, why?"

"The funny thing is, my pal, he started up his own practice a couple of years ago in another town on the coast – can't remember the name. If you needed a job, I'm sure he'd love to have you. The locals are a bit of a drawback – you know not exactly top-notch legal brains. He's trying to create a classy firm, the sort of thing you're used to."

A chord struck.

"What's your friend's name?"

"Simon. Simon Oakridge. He's a damn good sort. A real pal. Whatever job offer you have, it would be worth looking him up. A whole other level from some small-town outfit."

Yolanda suppressed her smile, recalling her impressions of Simon Oakridge and his vision. She remembered Mark's pals.

"How about it?"

She looked into his wide-open eyes with their sooty lashes, but the spell was broken.

"I've got a lot to do. To get settled. I'm not really looking for a relationship at the moment."

Mark sighed.

"It was worth a try. Good luck Yolanda."

When he'd gone, she suddenly had a longing. For a quiet man with no extravagant good looks, but a gentle, sensitive face.

Wearing a hat and oversized waistcoat. She knew Pete had done nothing wrong. Jackie's poison had nearly taken hold, but in the end, she'd failed.

◆ ◆ ◆

For the next few weeks, Yolanda's spare time was occupied with sorting out her belongings. She decided what to take, gave the rest to charity shops and slowly packed. She often spoke to Robin and the others in the evenings when they were in the pub. They told her Melody was getting better and hoping to come back soon.

"What're you going to do about moving your stuff?" Robin said, "Tash hired a van and we helped her load and unload it."

"I think I'm going to book a removal company."

"That'll be pricey."

Robin was right. Yolanda was shocked at the quotes she received from London removal companies. However, she didn't like asking for favours and didn't want to take advantage of her new friends. 'Frugal Living', had advice to offer – use a local company. She tried a few small firms in east Kent, and found one that wasn't as expensive as the rest. The guy said they had a small local job to do first on the day she was moving, but would be with her mid-morning. She was concerned about the vague timing, but the price was good.

Robin offered to come over after work and help Yolanda unpack on the Thursday – the day she was moving.

"No, thanks, I've got everything under control. I'm just planning to unpack a few things. I'll do the rest over the weekend. You could come and help then, if you don't mind. But I'll be fine by myself the first night."

The evening before her move, Yolanda spoke to Robin when she was in the pub. Everyone was excited.

"I can't wait," said Robin, "don't you feel like you're coming home?

CHAPTER 11

The moving day didn't go according to plan. Yolanda was up early and ready to go by nine. The removal company weren't due to arrive till mid-morning, but what did that mean? Everything was packed and all the boxes were labelled. It shouldn't take long to load up the van.
The kettle and tea things were packed away so Yolanda drank water from the tap. She sat on the sofa and checked Instagram. It seemed a long time later that she surfaced, but it was just after ten. She sighed and put her feet up. She jumped up at every noise – was that them? By eleven thirty, she began to worry. Had there been a mix-up? She checked her emails. Yes, both parties had confirmed the arrangements. It was still mid-morning, so vague. She wished she'd pushed them for a definite time.

She rang the removal van at twelve. Apparently, they were on their way, but wouldn't commit to an arrival time. The doorbell rang at one thirty, by which time Yolanda was thoroughly fed up. Loading the van took far longer than she expected, and the way the men chucked around the boxes, she was glad she didn't have any valuable china. She hoped her furniture would survive the move. Finally, everything was packed and she stood in the empty flat. It was strange and lonely.

The foreman told Yolanda they'd stop for lunch on the way, and they'd see her in a couple of hours at her new flat. She got in the car and went on her way. Crossing the QE 2 bridge always gave her a lift, and tired and hungry as she was, she felt better.

Pulling into her own parking space in the quiet Westgate square, Yolanda felt a thrill. She climbed the stairs to the first floor and put her key in the lock. She was home. Even though it was empty, the flat was bright and welcoming. She brought her bags up from the car and sat down on the floor to wait. However, this time the van arrived before expected. The removal men were keen to finish the job, and worked quickly. They dumped everything except the bed in thc lounge. She insisted they move the wardrobe and chest of drawers into the bedroom, but the men grumbled under their breath and she couldn't bear them around any longer.

It was now dark, and the mound of boxes in the lounge overwhelmed her. What'd she done? She'd never get straight. The doorbell rang. She opened the door, and there stood Pete. He was holding a plant in one hand and a bottle of wine in the other.

"I know you said you didn't want anyone around tonight. I thought I'd just bring you a pizza and go, but I don't know what you like. There's a place around the corner that'll deliver straightaway. If you want..."

Yolanda looked at him standing there with an anxious expression, as if unsure of his welcome. Unable to speak or move, to her horror, tears rolled down her cheeks.

"I'm sorry, I didn't mean to... I'll go..."

"No," she found the words, "please stay. It's been a hell of a day. I haven't eaten since... I can't remember."

"Okay, first thing pizza." He rang the number and turned to her, "what toppings?"

"Mushroom and onion."

He repeated this into the phone.

"Small or large ?"

"Large," she said, "you are staying?"

After the pizza and wine out of paper cups, Yolanda felt better and a little lightheaded.

"Pete, you're an angel."

He looked embarrassed, but pleased.

"Do you need help getting anything straight tonight?"

"No, I'll manage. I didn't plan to unpack in a hurry. I've got time – all tomorrow and the weekend."

Pete stood up.

"I'll be going."

She smiled a tired smile.

"Thanks so much for the pizza, wine, plant – and everything."

◆ ◆ ◆

By Sunday evening, with Robin's help, Yolanda's new flat was fully functioning, everything in its place and a warm welcoming feel. The next morning, she was to start her new job. Pete rang to wish her luck.

At her London firm, although the working day officially started at nine, anyone who wasn't at their desk by eight thirty was regarded as late. Yolanda arrived at the office in Ramsgate just before eight thirty. The entrance was through a shopfront, a couple of streets back from the sea. The door was locked and there was no sign of life. She wandered up the street looking at the other shops, while keeping an eye out to see if anyone opened the door. After fifteen minutes, a guy who looked as if he was barely out of his teens, arrived with a bunch of keys. He suggested she sit down in the waiting area.

No one else came until, on the dot of nine, a woman in a grey suit and lilac blouse entered. She was in her forties, with a pleasant face and simple, short hairstyle.

"Good morning, Darren. Ah, you must be Yolanda." she held out a hand. "Stella Pritchard, pleased to meet you." Her handshake was firm. "Come upstairs with me."

Stella took Yolanda into her office and made her a cup of tea. They both sat down.

"I'm a partner in the firm, and I'll be your mentor and line manager." Stella smiled at Yolanda. "We're very pleased you're joining us. Anything you want to know, come to me. It isn't easy starting somewhere new. There're two other lawyers at this branch as well as Darren and May who deal with reception and switchboard." She looked at Yolanda with a puzzled expression.

"Haven't I seen you before somewhere? Now where was it? Tash – were you at Tash's barbecue a few weeks ago?"

"Yes, she's one of the first people I met down here. How do you know her?"

"We both sing in the same choir, Roger Baldwin's wife Marion's the choir leader. By the way, do you sing? We're always looking for new members."

"My voice wouldn't be an asset to your choir," said Yolanda with a grin.

"When the others arrive, I'll introduce you." Stella rose "I'll show you your office." She led the way into a small, but bright room, overlooking the street. On the desk was a pile of files.

"Don't get a shock," said Stella, "I thought it would be a good idea for you to look through the files your predecessor was working on, familiarise yourself with the cases. Take a few days if necessary. Remember to ask me if you need anything." With a smile she left the room.

Later Yolanda met Brian who was Stella's age, and seemed friendly. Lisa, the other lawyer was just back from maternity leave, and only worked part time. She looked tired and anxious, but managed a smile.

Pete rang to ask how her first day had gone.

“It's early days, but it seems good so far. I'm tired so I won't go to the pub tonight, hopefully tomorrow.”

There was a pause.

“Would you like to go out for a meal on Saturday night?”

“Yes, I’d love to.”

◆ ◆ ◆

On Tuesday night, Yolanda went to the pub and the others quizzed her about the job. Melody was there, but a different Melody. She was thinner, but smiled and talked a lot.

“Lovely to see you again, Yolanda. Now you're really one of us.”

All traces of animosity had vanished.

Yolanda’s working week carried on in the same way it’d started. Contrary to Stella’s words, she was so used to working under pressure, she finished studying the case files in record time. On Thursday, Roger Baldwin came into her office.

“How’re you getting on? I've heard good reports from Stella already. I hope you'll be happy in our little band. By the way, Marion’s been nagging me to ask you over for dinner, we must make a date.”

The friendliness she received from everyone warmed Yolanda’s heart. She’d definitely made the right decision.

◆ ◆ ◆

On Saturday morning after breakfast, the doorbell rang. Yolanda opened the door to face a huge bouquet of flowers.

“These can't be for me.”

A muffled voice from behind the flowers confirmed her name, and handed them over. There was a note attached.

To my best girl,

Wishing you luck in your new home,

Love Tony.

How kind of him. Tears pricked her eyes.

She only had a couple of small vases, so she put the bouquet in a bucket.

She phoned Tony right away.

"Thanks so much. I don't know what to say... the flowers are gorgeous. I'll send you a picture."

"How're you doing, lass? How's it all going? New job, new home? That's a lot to take on."

Encouraged by the genuine concern and enthusiasm in his voice, Yolanda poured out everything that'd happened since she last saw him. Well not quite everything. She left out all mention of Pete. When she told him about Jackie's attempt to stop her renting out the London flat, he was shocked but not surprised.

"I said, didn't I, she'll stop at nothing."

"Has Mum said anything to you about me?"

"She knows you've moved – she didn't hear that from me – I don't know how she's found out the details."

Yolanda didn't reply immediately.

"I think she's using a private investigator."

"That wouldn't surprise me, I'm sorry, lass."

"I wonder what else she'll do..."

"You haven't heard then?"

"Heard what?"

"I don't want this hanging over you. I don't care if it's supposed to be a secret. You know Jackie's always wanted to do business in America?"

Yolanda didn't expect this.

"Yes, she's talked about it for years – breaking into the American market. But she never had the right contacts."

"She has now. For the past year or so, she's had someone out there looking. He found a salon in Florida. It's run down and she can get it cheap. George went out with her to look at it. It's all they talk about. Going over the numbers. You know how they love that kind of thing. I'm bored stiff with it. All this money, they don't enjoy it. You've got the right idea, love.

"They've been working on the deal for months and she wasn't sure it would come to anything. But just this week she's signed the contract. She's got a good manager looking after the salons here and she's off to America soon as possible to get started."

This was something to think about.

"Don't you see, lass, this is Jackie's dream come true. What she's always wanted. She's got bigger fish to fry now – she'll leave you alone."

Yes, petty harassment of her daughter wouldn't be a priority.

"Don't say anything about this. I'm just telling you so you can stop worrying."

"Of course, Tony. It's a big relief. Thanks, you're an angel."

"Never mind about that, you take care of yourself, my girl. And keep in touch."

Yolanda took a while to digest the news. She looked at the bouquet of flowers sitting in the bucket. Tony's thoughtful gift deserved to be properly displayed. But where could she get a vase that wasn't too expensive? She remembered passing a charity shop in the High Street, surely, she could find something suitable there. A few minutes later, she was outside the shop.

Inside, she found an area devoted to vases, ornaments and crockery. The vases were too small, but Yolanda spotted a large glass jug that would fit the bill. She carried it over to the till, where a young woman was folding clothes. She put the jug down and waited. On the wall behind the counter, several of the ubiquitous seascapes hung. She squinted at a painting of a horse. There was something wrong with the proportions or perspective. She looked at the next picture. Her heart rose inside her chest and then plummeted. It couldn't be... but it was. The portrait of Beth. Margery's portrait of Beth – the one from the Airbnb. What was it doing in a charity shop?

The shop assistant completed her task and smiled.

"The jug's three pounds fifty, please. Would you like a bag?"

Yolanda's mouth was dry. She pointed at the portrait.

"That picture... where did you get it from?"

The woman frowned and turned her head.

"Somebody brought it in a few days ago. Do you like it?" she asked eagerly.

Once again, Yolanda's eyes were drawn to the eyes in the portrait. The effect was as strong as before. The enigmatic expression as devastating. Once again, she wondered, was it pain, terror, misery? She felt dizzy.

"Are you alright, love? Here, sit down." The assistant pulled out a chair from behind the counter. "I'll get you some water."

Yolanda gulped it down.

"I'm not surprised you feel bad," said the assistant, looking over at the picture. "I can't stand the sight of it. I'm sure it'll never sell. More likely to drive customers away. I didn't want to take it, but we can't turn away donations."

"But who brought it, why?" asked Yolanda in a weak voice.

The assistant frowned.

"A woman...She said it was from a rental. Someone complained about it – said it scared their kids."

"How much is it?"

"Five pounds. But you don't want to buy it? You went quite white before."

"I'm not sure."

"Well, it's up to you. We're always glad of a sale."

Yolanda didn't want the picture, but she couldn't leave it there. It wasn't right – in that dusty shop among those banal, unwanted items. In the end, she handed over the five pounds and left the shop with the picture wrapped in newspaper, and the jug in a large bag.

Back in her flat, she unwrapped the picture and shrank back, trembling. She'd forgotten how profoundly Beth's portrait had affected her. Now it was even stronger. The connection between the two of them was almost tangible. Beth's eyes beseeched, implored, tore at Yolanda's heart.

"What do you want?" she cried aloud.

And then the realisation. It was about that night, the night Beth disappeared. Something had happened to her. She'd been destroyed, and she couldn't rest. All these years later, she was reaching out for help. Yolanda whispered.

"What can I do?"

And immediately into her brain came the answer.

"Take away my pain."

"How?"

"When the time comes, you'll know."

Beth's eyes released Yolanda as if a bond had been cut. A spell broken. She stood there breathing heavily. With a quick movement, she lifted the painting and turning the face to the wall, pushed it behind the sofa. She sat down and waited for her heart to stop racing.

◆ ◆ ◆

Yolanda felt drained. Lethargic. This wasn't like her. She'd had a lot of upheaval recently; they say moving house is stressful, and a new job. What would improve her mood? The sea. Of course, she'd go for a walk by the sea. It was cloudy, with a fresh breeze and she set off, eager to get to know the sea in all its moods.

The beach was almost deserted, although a couple of hardy souls sat outside Pav's. The sea rolled out in many shades of grey, matching Yolanda's mood. She walked close to the water's edge, breathing in its fresh briny tang. The wide empty horizon allowed her mind to relax. The rhythmic sound of the waves swept away tension. In half an hour, with face glowing from the wind and body calmed by the exercise, she returned to the flat.

She opened her wardrobe. What should she wear tonight? Pete had never seen her dressed up. She took her time, scrutinising the clothes and accessories, trying out different effects. Yolanda wondered where he'd take her. She felt a pleasurable ripple of anticipation. Their first proper date. Would he wear his usual combination of hat and waistcoat? She was used to his unique style and couldn't imagine him dressed in anything else. If he wore a suit and tie, she probably wouldn't recognise him.

The doorbell rang. Yolanda checked her reflection in the mirror and opened it. Pete stood there, with his gentle smile. His eyes widened.

"You look gorgeous." He looked round the room. "You've done a great job, it's a lovely flat."

He went over to the enormous bouquet on the table, picked up the card and frowned.

"Who's Tony?"

With a tiny thrill, she saw he was jealous.

"He's my – I suppose he's my dad, in a way."

Pete looked relieved but surprised.

"What do you mean?"

"I never knew my dad. My mum brought me up by herself, but

she worked long hours, she's very ambitious. I was alone a lot. Tony's married to my mum's best friend. They didn't have any kids. He was the only one I could talk to, who understood me. Who wanted to understand me."

"The flowers are beautiful. They must've cost a lot. He must have plenty of money."

"His wife, she has a dress shop in Leeds, a really successful business. Tony's a carpenter. He's kind and down to earth. You'd like him."

As he drove, Pete continued the conversation.

"It must be awkward, if one partner has a lot more money than the other."

"I don't know, I think it comes down to values and expectations."

They drove out of Westgate down dark country lanes; Yolanda had no idea where they were going. They arrived at a small village, and pulled up outside a pub.

"Someone told me about this place," said Pete, "otherwise you'd never know it was here."

The White Horse Inn was everything the name implied. Old, full of character, with an interesting menu written in chalk on a board. They sat at a table in the corner, a little way from the other diners. Yolanda looked at Pete properly. He wore a grey tweed waistcoat with a subtle check and a white shirt. His flat cap had a pronounced peak. It reminded her of something.

"*Peaky Blinders,*" she said, "you look like the guy in *Peaky Blinders*. Have you watched it?"

"No, what's it about?"

"A gang. You look like the gang leader."

"Really? What kind of person is he?"

"Ruthless – but sort of attractive and stylish."

He considered her words.

"That doesn't sound too bad – apart from the ruthless."

She smiled. "You should watch it. The filming is interesting, dark and moody with a twist."

The food was good and service discreet.

"You wouldn't expect to find a place as good as this in the middle of nowhere," said Yolanda.

Pete smiled and refilled her glass. She looked at his hands. They weren't much larger than hers, the fingers slim. The sensitive hands of an artist. He noticed her gaze and put his hands in his lap. After an excellent sticky toffee pudding, she sat back with a sigh.

"That was the best meal I've had in a long time. Thanks Pete."

He looked at her, then brought something out of his pocket. He put a small package wrapped in tissue paper on the table in front of her.

"A gift."

She removed the paper to reveal a white box with 'Madi' in gold letters. She opened it. Inside lay a pair of earrings. The clear drops shimmered with metallic fragments, catching the light.

"They're beautiful."

"I made them specially for you. I noticed you had pierced ears. It's a new design I'm trying out."

She put the earrings on. "How do they look?"

"Perfect."

The waiter arrived with coffee.

As they walked to the car, Pete took Yolanda's hand.

"Back to your place?"

"Yes. Would you like to come in for a drink?"

◆ ◆ ◆

"What do you want to drink, I've got wine, whisky, brandy?"

"A small whisky please."

While she was getting the drinks, Pete pulled the painting out from behind the sofa.

"What's this?"

He turned the picture round, propped it against the wall and stood back. Yolanda put the drinks down.

"It's a portrait of the girl I was looking for. The one that disappeared. Something about it haunted me. I wanted to find out what happened to her."

"What was the girl's name?" he asked.

"It was Beth, Beth Winthrop."

Pete stared at the picture as if transfixed. His face was white.

"Beth," he repeated, "it's Beth." He sat down on the sofa, picked up the whisky and drained the glass. His hands were shaking. He stood up.

"I didn't realise. I can't – I'm sorry..."

He stared at the picture, as if he was frozen. Then he rushed out of the front door. Yolanda heard his rapid footsteps going down the stairs.

CHAPTER 12

What was the matter with him? Had she said something, done something? But Yolanda knew she was avoiding the truth. It was the painting. Beth's anguished expression that affected her so viscerally, must've done the same to Pete. She shook her head. No, not just the picture. It was more than that. The name. When she said Beth's name, that was what upset him.
Why? Don't ask, don't go there. This can't end well.

She forced herself to think back to the earlier part of the evening. Everything was fine, they were relaxed, having a good time. When she asked Pete in for a drink and he agreed, she thought perhaps he'd stay. She hoped...

He liked her; she knew he did. But to go off like that, without a word. He looked as if he'd seen a ghost. Was that Beth? Was she the ghost? Yolanda had to find out, but at the same time fear drew her back. She tried to close her mind, but ideas and images forced their way in.

"I don't want to know," she said out loud. Saying the words made it worse, admitting there was something to know. Something hidden, a secret.

She shivered. She poured a glass of wine and wrapped herself in a blanket. She must face it. But maybe it wasn't that bad... maybe there was an explanation. Whichever way she looked at it the inevitable answer stared her in the face, Pete knew something about Beth. About her disappearance.

Yolanda's stomach churned; fear gnawed at her. Fear for Pete, for herself.

Maybe he'd come back and explain. Curled up on the sofa, she waited. Every so often she looked at her phone – nothing. She wasn't yet accustomed to the usual noises of her neighbours and the area outside. Nerves strained, she started at every sound. Was that Pete coming back? No. The time dragged by.

Surely he would explain, would phone, however upset he was. It wasn't like him. But how well did she really know him? Perhaps not as well as she thought. Her heart ached. Everything was going wrong. Maybe coming to live here was a huge mistake, maybe Jackie was right. No. Don't go down that path, there must be an explanation for Pete's distress.

Then the doorbell rang. Yolanda's heart pounded so hard her whole body shook. She crept over to the door and slowly opened it, peering round into the landing.

Pete stood there. His face was deathly pale, the features drawn.

"I'm sorry. I want to explain. Please can I come in?"

She opened the door without a word. They sat down in the lounge.

"Could I have a whisky?" She brought him a glass and he sipped it. He took a deep breath.

Yolanda sat on a stool where she could see him. His face was ashen, his teeth clenched, and he was holding the glass so tightly his knuckles were white. He sat rigidly as if gripped by a strong emotion. She didn't know what to say or do.

"Pete, are you..?"

He tried to speak, but no words came out.

"Are you okay? Can I do anything?"

"No," he said finally, in a trembling voice, "I'm alright. There's something – something I have to say, tell you... I knew I'd have to sometime, but I hoped... I've been putting it off."

She looked at him helplessly.

"What?"

"It's about Beth," he said, and drank a mouthful of whisky. "I have to tell you what happened."

He swallowed the rest of the whisky in one gulp. He coughed, but his face regained its colour. The next words came more freely.

"I'm from Chelmsford. The same street as her. We were about seven or eight when we met. Both quiet. Beth's mum and dad didn't like me. They thought she should have a crowd of girlfriends. Laughing and making a noise, like Karen. The perfect daughter." He paused. "But Beth just had me.

"I could tell even then she wasn't happy. She was different from the rest of the family. Didn't fit in. They were always on at her to cheer up. As if it was that simple. Brett made fun of her. Her mum and dad asked why she was miserable. But not like they cared. More like they were blaming her for spoiling their perfect, happy family. They never really tried to find out... To help."

"She knew there was something wrong. They'd be better off without her. I was the only one she could talk to. I listened, but I couldn't help.

"School was difficult, specially secondary school. Beth was an outsider there as well. The others ignored her or picked on her. There were some boys – real bullies. She couldn't concentrate. Did badly.

"She started wearing big, loose clothes. They made her feel safe. It was the same with her hair. She could hide behind it."

Pete stopped talking. He licked his lips and asked for a glass of water. Yolanda's heart was thumping. Where was this leading? He went on.

"She did have a couple of other friends for a while. Like her. Misfits. They understood how she felt. But her family called them weirdos. Made fun of them.

"The rows at home got worse. With her dad. She should pull herself together. She was wasting her life. On and on. Her mum was only interested in Karen – her wedding."

Pete drew his breath in sharply. He picked up the whisky glass, but it was empty. Silently Yolanda refilled it and he drank.

"That was the worst row. Before the wedding. Beth was supposed to be a bridesmaid. She wouldn't even try on the dress. Her dad was shouting. Her mum started crying...

"In the end, Beth went into the bathroom and vomited until her stomach was empty. Until she was dizzy. And she realised. Understood the reason for everything. She hated her body. Couldn't stand the sight or feel of it. The thought of it being on show in a tight-fitting dress was unbearable."

While he was talking, Pete stared into the distance as if he was describing a film unfolding in front of his eyes. He went on.

"That was the first time she thought about suicide. It seemed the only way out. How else could she escape from her own body? The idea terrified her, but so did the thought of living.

"She left school, but could only get dead-end jobs. She struggled along like a sleepwalker stuck in a nightmare. Suicide didn't seem so bad.

"At that time, the only thing that helped was walking. We walked for hours in the evenings. In quiet streets. Away from crowds. Then something happened." He paused.

"It was dark. We turned a corner and there they were. The boys from school. They stood there blocking our way. Looking at Beth. Laughing."

His voice faltered.

"Freak. Queer. Lezza." He whispered, shrinking back in his seat.

"Hands reaching…"

Yolanda gasped.

"We ran… We got away."

His head dropped into his hands.

Yolanda's pent-up breath escaped in a sigh.

Pete raised his head.

"Beth was in shock. She didn't tell anyone what happened, but she stayed in her room for days. She began to wonder if the bullies were right. Was she gay? Was that why she felt so bad about her body?

"We were in her room and she was staring at herself in the mirror. I watched her reflection. She had the same look on her face as in that portrait. Tormented. Desperate.

"I couldn't stand it. I had to tell her. Although it was hard to say, I forced myself. I couldn't say it out loud, so I whispered into her ear. And waited.

"I was sure she would react. Her head went down so her hair covered her face, but she didn't say anything. Not then or afterwards. Things carried on the same as before.

"In the summer she was desperate to get away. Anywhere. In the end, she went to Broadstairs with Amber. From the start they didn't get on. They had nothing in common. The first night a couple of guys started chatting them up in the pub. Amber was all over one and the other flirted with Beth.

"She tried to ignore him, hiding behind her hair, but he took no notice. He pushed her hair away and leaned over. Right up close. Grinning. She was going to vomit. She had to get away.

"Outside the streets were full of people. She pushed her way towards the sea. Walked along the beach. Away from the lights and noise. She shouldn't've come. It was a mistake. Her thoughts went round and round. No hope. No way out. This was the end. She went down to the edge of the sea.

"The sky and water were dark. But as she stood there, the moon came out. It lit a path across the sea. A way out.

"The waves were cold and her jeans dragged her down. She struggled on, one footstep at a time. Until she heard the voices. They were all around her, shrieking and splashing. Like she was in hell. She turned round and waded back to the shore.

"Back at the pub, the gig had finished and Amber was gone. Beth walked back to the campsite and crawled into her sleeping bag.

"The next day she was worn out. There were crowds and noise everywhere and she followed Amber around in a daze. They ended up in another pub in the evening. But the night turned out differently.

"The performer, Jango James, started with a couple of well-known folk songs. The audience was quiet. Beth relaxed.

"Jango wasn't a great singer or musician, but something in his performance got to her. For the first time, she thought about what I'd told her. The knowledge she'd buried. The song was called 'Now Is the Time'. She couldn't make out all the words, but what she did hear hit home. Unlocking something inside her. Questions she hadn't dared to ask. And answers."

Now Pete was breathing heavily, his chest heaving.

"For the first time in her life she felt hope. Her heart opened. Just a little.

"The next night Jango was performing at a different pub. Amber agreed to go. He played most of the songs from the day before, but not the one Beth wanted to hear. It was almost the end of his set. She forced herself to go over and ask him to play it. When he played the song she found more questions. And answers.

"The next day, Amber made it clear Beth wasn't playing her part. Not doing what Amber expected. And she said she wasn't going to spend every night listening to Jango James. So, they went their separate ways. Beth went to a morning session Jango was playing at a café, and heard the song again.

"As she always did, Beth confided in me. We were in touch every day. She told me what was happening and how she felt. I could sense her excitement. A tone in her voice I'd never heard before. Hope. I was excited as well. This was so important, I wanted to be there with her. So, I came. To Broadstairs.

"I was in the pub that night. The night she heard Jango sing the song for the last time. Beth was already there when I arrived. The pub was crowded and she didn't see me. Jango began to sing."

Pete sang, almost in a whisper,

"Now is the time..."

He went on,

"I watched Beth. She was staring at Jango. I watched her expression. Her eyes got wider and wider. It was like she saw a beautiful vision. She was really happy. She sat up straight and shook her hair back out of her face. I'd never seen her like that before.

"When the song finished, she stood up, as if she was in a dream. She walked out of the pub; her head held high. Glad to be alive.

"Beth hadn't seen me and I didn't want to disturb her in that state. I picked up my rucksack and followed her out of the pub. She walked down the street ignoring the crowds. She went on and on to the edge of the town, and then into the countryside. There was no one else around. I walked behind her, keeping my distance, I didn't want to alarm her. She went off the road into a field. I followed her.

"She suddenly stopped. As if she sensed something. She turned round and saw me. 'It's you'. She looked into my face and I saw she finally understood.

'Pete, the song... it helped me see what I have to do. I've felt like this for so long. There was something wrong with me. Really wrong. Even when you told me. I couldn't take it in. But you knew, didn't you? You've always known.'

"She was right. I'd always known because I started it. I made her different. I didn't mean to. I tried to stop myself, to fight against my feelings. But they were too strong. She wanted to get away, escape from me. She never did.

"Pete and Beth, Beth and Pete, I thought we'd always be together. But now she'd realised. We stood there facing each other in that field, in the bright moonlight. I stared into her eyes. We couldn't be together. Never again. That was over.

I knew what I had to do. I took off my rucksack."

Icy hands clawed at Yolanda's heart. She cried out.

"Why're you telling me this... I don't understand?"

"I have to... Even though you'll never want to see me again. Or have anything to do with me. You'll be shocked, disgusted."

He couldn't look her in the face, he was shaking.

"Then why...?"

"Because it's part of me – who I am."

"No, I don't need to hear this. I don't care. Don't say any more..."

"I must. You must know the truth. I can't keep this to myself any longer. I know I'm destroying everything between us. But it's too big. Too important. I can't hide this from you. Please, listen..."

If only he would stop. If the words weren't spoken – the act not named – there was still hope for them. They could be together. She could push the terrible thoughts out of her mind. But once he said the words, they could never be unsaid or forgotten. His words would rip them apart forever. But the pain in his voice was unbearable. She said no more. He went on.

"I opened my rucksack. There were the scissors. The sharp, shiny scissors. Beth stood still. She was waiting. She wanted me to do it. To set her free."

Yolanda wept, hiding her face in her hands. Her brain was a confused mass of thoughts and images. As Pete told his story, her mind leapt to the only possible ending. There could be no other outcome. He had killed Beth. He was a murderer. Those were the facts. And by those facts, light and hope were extinguished from her life.

"I said Beth's name for the last time. I reached over and stroked her hair. Her thick, heavy, curly hair. The scissors were bright, glittering in the moonlight. That night in the field, that was the last night. The end of Beth.

"Finally, I was alone. Beth was gone. I stood there for a while without moving. The wind blew my hair. My long, thick, curly hair."

Yolanda looked at him. Uncomprehending.

"I took the scissors. The shining scissors and I cut. I cut and cut and cut. Until it was all gone. The hair was gone. At last, I was free. There was no more Beth. There was only Pete."

"What do you mean, what are you saying?"

He had stopped shaking. He looked Yolanda in the face. Now he'd come this far, he was strangely calm.

"I mean, I was Beth. And now I'm Pete. We're the same person."

Yolanda said nothing. Her mind was in turmoil. She couldn't process his words.

"I don't understand..."

He continued in the same calm voice.

"From a young age, Beth was aware of Pete. He was someone special, an invisible friend. She told him everything. Later, she realised he only existed inside her own head. But as she grew up, Pete took over more and more of that headspace.

"When she reached puberty, she felt more comfortable dressing as Pete, in loose tee shirts and jeans. She hated wearing girl's clothes, feeling ridiculous, like she was wearing bizarre, outrageous fancy dress. She knew this wasn't normal. She was in so much mental pain there had to be something really wrong.

But she had no one to help her. Sometimes death seemed the only way out.

"As I said, she wondered if she was gay, but that answer didn't feel right. I told her the truth, but the idea was so impossible... It couldn't be true.

"When she heard the words of the song, 'Now Is the Time', at Folk Week, something happened. For the first time she had the courage to face the hidden part of herself. She finally understood. She was Pete – a boy – but she'd been born into the wrong body. Beth's body.

"As she heard the song again and again, she began to see a way out of her misery. A way to become her true self. She could try and become Pete, at least outwardly. That's what happened that night in the field."

"I thought, I thought..." Yolanda moaned.

Then the rush of realisation. She thought Pete was a murderer – that he'd killed Beth. But he hadn't. That was all she cared about. He hadn't murdered Beth. He hadn't done anything wrong.

Pete sat on the sofa in a rigid, awkward position, waiting for her reaction. Yolanda looked into his face and caught her breath. The expression in his eyes. She knew it. The anguish, terror... But this time it was worse, far worse than before. From Pete's face, Beth's eyes looked at her, held her in a final, frantic grasp. Again, the words.

"Take away my pain. Now is the time."

Yolanda saw the agony in Pete's face and her heart leapt.

"I love you, Pete," she said. As the words came out of her mouth, she knew they were true.

Pete didn't react. What she said didn't register. As if in a trance, he sat stiffly on the sofa, his hands gripping his knees. Under the peak of his cap, his face was white, the features set into a mask.

Yolanda went to Pete and knelt down beside him. Leaning

forward, she reached over and took his face in her hands. She gently lifted his chin. His eyes met hers and she flinched at their raw pain. Slowly and deliberately, she kissed him.

His lips were cold and unresponsive. Surely, she hadn't made a mistake. Misread him? But after a moment – an endless moment – he came to life. His arms went round her and they held each other, not moving, for a long time. When they drew apart, Yolanda looked into Pete's eyes again. With a joyous throb of her heart, she saw he was at peace. That terrible haunting look had gone. She'd driven it away.

"I love you, Pete." she said again.

He looked at her – no longer with terror, but with uncertainty, apprehension, incredulity.

"Are you sure? Do you really understand? I'm not..."

"I don't care about the past."

She could say that now. Now she knew he hadn't done that thing, that terrible thing. Her heart was light, free. She took his hands and looked straight into his eyes.

"More sure than I've ever been in my life."

Emotionally drained, exhausted, but happy, they sat with their arms around each other for a long time.

"I know what we need now," said Yolanda, trying to sound matter of fact, "a cup of tea. You stay here I'll make it."

The tea revived them.

"Can I tell you the rest, what happened after...?"

"Are you sure you want to, now?"

"Yes, I want you to know everything. It'll be such a relief."

She nodded.

"After my hair was gone. I felt incredible. Free, lightheaded – as if I could fly away into the moonlight. I was truly myself. It was a kind of ecstasy. Rebirth.

"I lay down under the trees and went to sleep. When I woke up, I remembered what'd happened. What I'd done. My head felt different, but I touched my hair to make sure. It was gone. But so was the excitement and joy of the night before. Without my hair, really being Pete for the first time was frightening. I felt exposed. I had no shield. I didn't know what to do.

"After a while, I dug a hole in the earth with my hands, and buried my hair. I turned off my phone and buried that as well. Then in a kind of daze I stood up. I had one thought in my mind, to find protection. I walked back into the town. The streets were already busy. Nobody paid attention to me, just another androgynous figure in the crowd. I went into a charity shop and picked up a hat, a man's hat and put it on. Right away I felt better, safer. I put a waistcoat on over my tee shirt. It hid my body. I was okay.

I bought some food and then I had to get away – I couldn't risk bumping into Amber. I went back the way I'd come. Back into the country. Not into the field, but along the roads. I walked on and on. I must've slept rough for a while, I don't remember.

After a couple of days, I was still in this area, I must've been going in circles. I came to a small lane and something made me turn into it. There were no houses. I walked to the end and there was a cottage with a shed in the garden. Somewhere to sleep. I crept past the cottage. A window was open and I heard the sound of someone crying. I knocked at the front door, but nothing happened. Round the back, a door was unlocked and I went inside.

"The crying was coming from a room with an open door. There was a woman in bed. She asked me to help her and I did the best I could. She thanked me and smiled.

"I felt strange. Something happened in my head. This woman was looking at me with gratitude. Approval. I couldn't remember anyone looking at me like that before.

"I saw the lines of pain cut into her face; her lips squeezed together to stop a cry escaping. I forgot myself, all my problems and misery. I helped her wash her face, and made her some food.

She told me she'd lived there alone for a long time, but she'd never been lonely. She'd been in pain a great deal, but never cried out like that before. And then I came. Once again, that look. Acceptance. I found out her name was Madi and she had arthritis, which flared up more and more often. I stayed. I felt like I'd come home. Someone needed me.

"When a policeman came inquiring about Beth, Madi told him I was her son. She never asked me any questions.

"Madi told me I should let my parents know I was alright. It took a while, but I wrote a letter. I put in some things I'd always wanted to say. They wouldn't come looking for me after that."

Yolanda remembered the tears in Phil's eyes. But this wasn't the time.

Madi had lived in the cottage alone for years. She had a jewellery business, she designed and made everything herself. But now with the arthritis, sometimes she could hardly move. I took care of her when she felt bad, and looked after the cottage. She showed me how to make the jewellery, and I had a flair for the work. Before I came, she'd been worried the business would fail when she was ill, but now her mind was at rest.

Madi had no family. She'd never been married and had no children. She was so good to me, so caring and kind. She was my real mother."

Pete sighed deeply. He hadn't finished but seemed reluctant to go on.

"And after a while, Madi found me a doctor. A sympathetic, understanding doctor who agreed to help me. The hormone treatment began. A long, difficult time of transition.

Madi got worse, couldn't work at all. We also found out she had a serious heart complaint. There was nothing they could do. She told me she'd come to think of me as her son." He gulped.

"It was still hard to believe that somebody wanted me... After everything that happened with my real, I mean my other family. She asked me if I'd take her surname, like we were really related." He stared into the distance, as if viewing a vivid memory. "I was proud to take her name. Also, it completed my transformation. I was a new person.

"I took over the business and developed it. And I looked after her until..." there was a catch in his voice, "until she passed away. That was the worst day of my life," Pete put his hands over his eyes, "I missed her so much.

He let out a deep breath and sank back in his seat.

"She left me the cottage and the business. I was okay, I made friends, but I never thought – never dreamed that I'd ever find someone. That anyone would want me."

The two of them sat together. Talking, asking questions. And not talking. Just glad to have found each other. Yolanda looked at Pete. She wished he'd take his hat off, so she could see him properly. But she sensed it was too soon, he wasn't ready to let down all his defences. She could be patient.

Pete stood up, "I'd better be going."

"Would you, stay tonight? Not... I don't mean.... Just to be near you."

He sat back down on the sofa and Yolanda nestled into his arms.

That was how she woke up. Pete was still asleep. In the night, his hat had fallen off and lay on the floor. Yolanda turned her head to look at him properly. His sandy hair was cut short. Sleeping, he looked younger. An overwhelming tenderness came over her, that brought tears to her eyes. She reached out and gently stroked his head. Pete opened his eyes. He looked surprised, as if wondering where he was. Then he smiled and drew Yolanda towards him.

ACKNOWLEDGEMENT

Thanks to Jackie Bates for editorial input.

Printed in Great Britain
by Amazon

85993756R00119